A Touch of Death

of Death

 Reaper: Book One

Marissa Dobson

Published by Sunshine Press

Printed in the United States of America

ISBN-13: 978-1-939978-38-7

Dedication

To Thomas, who spent countless hours helping me get this perfect. Not to mention the endless research he assisted with, not only for this book but also for future books in the Reaper series.

To my readers: I hope you enjoy this book as much as I enjoyed rewriting this series. Here's to the start of a whole *new* Reaper series.

The death of Jael James' mother meant it was time to face her destiny as the Grim Reaper. Her first spirit shows up after being murdered, demanding the killer be caught before she can cross over. If a serial killer on the loose wasn't bad enough, it turned out to be a demon sent by Lucifer to test her.

Death is there to guide her as she makes the journey into the unknown, but he seems to have his own agenda—which involves getting her naked. He wants to show her what they could have together. But then there's Nathan, who wants to be more than just her paramedic partner. Competing with Death for her attention might be more than Nathan can handle.

Will Jael find a balance that will keep her secret safe, or will her new role as Grim Reaper force her to walk away from the two most important men in her life?

Contents:

Prologue

Tears welled in Jael's eyes as she sat at her dying mother's bedside. As an adult it wasn't supposed to be this devastating to lose a parent. No longer would her mother suffer. She wouldn't have to put up with harsh criticism for talking to *people* no one else could see.

Jael rested her head against the back of the chair, the rough wood digging into her skull. The feeling grounded her, helped her force the tears back. Time with her mother was nearing its end, and she didn't want to waste it by crying. Opening her eyes, she saw a man leaning against the wall. Dressed in black, his jeans and T-shirt clung tight. His clothing was a dark contrast to his creamy white skin and the bright white wall behind him. His hair fell just above his ears, reminding her of spilled ink, a few stray pieces dangling just above his sapphire eyes that sparkled with hints of silver.

Drop dead gorgeous is an understatement. This was no time to let her hormones get out of control. Her mother needed her to remain focused.

"Can I help you?" She raised an eyebrow at him. There was no way he was medical staff. He continued to lean against the wall, completely ignoring her. Her unease rose, but instead of giving into it she pushed back from her chair and stood. "This is a private room and visiting hours are over. Please leave."

"I'm here to see her." He nodded toward her mother.

"She's not up for visitors now. If you could come back tomorrow maybe she'll be ready then." In no mood to deal with him, she reached to the side of the bed, her finger hovering just above the nurse call button.

"Ann." His voice floated through the room, with a hint of mystery.

She eyed him with anger for his lack of respect for her privacy. "I don't know how you know my mother, but I asked you to leave. Go or I'll call security."

A light chuckle teased the air. "I wouldn't recommend that."

"What's that supposed to mean?" she snapped.

"Jael?" Ann's eyes were glazed from the drugs that coursed through her body.

As if summoned by her mother's voice, the man moved away from the wall and came toward the bed. "Ann, it's time to tell her."

"No, not yet." Tears welled in Ann's eyes, as she tugged the breathing mask away from her face. "I need more time."

"I've given you as much time as I could, but it's nearly up. Don't make me deliver the news." With that he disappeared as quickly as he'd appeared. He just vanished. Jael startled, jumping back, then sinking into her chair, shocked and near panic.

"What the hell just happened?" She pinched herself to make sure it wasn't all a dream. She'd had so little sleep the last few days, she wouldn't have been surprised if she had dozed off or hallucinated the whole thing.

"Destiny has been revealed." Ann's breathy voice cut through Jael's thoughts.

"What?"

"I'm dying." When Jael started to interrupt, Ann shook her head to stop her. "Don't, just hear me out. It's going to sound bizarre so I need to say it *all* before you interrupt. All these years, people thought I was crazy, seeing people they don't. It's because I'm the Grim Reaper."

"The what?" Jael had been asked to keep quiet, but her heart was slamming against her chest, and she couldn't stop herself. "Mom, I think it's the drugs the doctor gave you. Please rest."

"It's not the drugs. If you trace our family history back, you'll see that the first female born in each generation has been given the ability to see the dead. We are the Grim Reaper. Without us, the spirits stuck in limbo cannot cross over into the light. It's our calling, our destiny. He will help you along your path, assist you with what you need." She gripped Jael's hand, taking a moment to catch her breath. "I've sheltered you while I could, but now that my time on this Earth is coming to an end, it's time for you to take my place."

She heard her mother's words but couldn't believe them. It had to be the medication that was making her delusional. Her mom had always been eccentric, talking to people no one else could see. But a

Grim Reaper? They didn't exist. When you died, there was no limbo, just Heaven or Hell, your body turning to dust in the ground, nothing more.

"Mom, just rest."

After years of being a paramedic in Crystal Falls, Montana, she had seen death more times than she cared to remember, and never once had a ghost risen out of a body asking for help. It just didn't happen. When someone died, there was nothing left for them in this world. Even if there was life after death, there was no room in Jael's life to help those who'd passed on. Death was already an unavoidable part of her job, but to see the spirits of those she couldn't save sounded like more than she could handle.

Why worry? I don't believe what she's saying anyway.

"You need to understand what will happen. Things will change for you when I die."

Jael squeeze her mother's hand. "It will be fine. There are always changes in life. Don't worry, I'll be fine. I'll miss you, but you'll be with Dad again. Everything is going to be fine."

"Your father…" Ann's smile was warm and wishful, as she reached her hand out to touch the length of something, but all Jael could see was thin air. "He's always been with me, but to actually touch him again will make up for leaving you. I've always wanted to protect you, Jael. I love you."

"I know, Mom. I love you too. Sleep, I'll figure everything out, it's going to be fine."

The drugs helping to lessen Ann's pain from the bone cancer were pulling her under again, sleep's long fingers reaching out to her to drag her under. In the back of Jael's mind, she wondered if this would be the last time her mother ever spoke to her. Ann had already lived two weeks past the doctor's expectation.

Unable to sit, she paced the room, her mind running in circles. She needed fresh air and wished she could open a window. With little choice she strolled into the bathroom, grabbed a paper towel, wet it, and placed it over her forehead. The coolness against her warm skin refreshed her. Now she hoped to find some strong, hot coffee to help get her through the night.

"Your mother told you what you are." Death leaned against the doorframe between her mother's room and the bathroom. His arms were crossed over his chest as he watched her. "I can unleash your powers and allow you to see across the planes to the land of the dead…if you're ready."

She threw the towel in the trash and brushed past him. "I'll never be ready. I don't want that life, find someone else."

"So you believe Ann, then?" The corner of his mouth tugged up in a smirk.

"Hell no! I mean…I don't know." She dragged her hand through her long blonde hair, unable to look at him. "Mom's was always been a little eccentric. If she truly believes she sees people others don't, then whatever, but I don't want to be a part of it. I don't want her life."

"It's your legacy. There is only one Grim Reaper at a time, and you're it. You will carry on the line when your mother passes, as your child will, and their child."

Spinning around, she glared at him. "Legacy? Why didn't she tell me about it before? How did she expect me to handle or believe it when it's dropped on me like this?"

"I didn't agree with Ann keeping this from you. You should have been told so you could have adjusted to it. As you aged she should have allowed me to unleash your powers slowly, giving you time to process everything and learn from her. Now you'll only have time for a crash course before you step into her place."

"I don't want this. To be seen as crazy as she was is no life. I have everything I want, a good job, a beautiful condo. Just leave me alone." She sank into the chair next to the hospital bed, tears streaming down her face.

"If I could give you that I would, but it's your legacy. You have no choice but to step into her place once she passes. I will return."

With the slightest breeze against the back of her neck, she knew he was gone. "I'd rather take your place, Mom, than live with this curse."

Chapter One

Slumber wrapped heavily around Jael like a familiar blanket. She wanted to roll over and go back to sleep, but something woke her. Nightmare? No. Alarm? No. That's when she smelled him. His cologne was unmistakable. It had planted itself firmly in her memory, so no matter what, she couldn't forget it. Almost like the man himself. She couldn't forget him, either.

In the month since the hospital visit, she had only seen him in the distance at the funeral. He observed but didn't stick around after the services to speak with her. When she asked her best friend, Gemma, what happened to the man in the black on black suit, Gemma's perplexed expression gave her the answer. No one else had seen him.

It was impossible Gemma would have missed him, because he was standing directly across from them, just beyond the coffin. Jael thought back to his first visit and how he'd appeared out of thin air. It was too much for her to take in. None of it should have been possible.

"Jael, darling. We need to speak," he said from what sounded like the foot of her bed.

"Not now. I worked the night shift, go away, I need my beauty sleep." She grabbed a pillow and threw it at him, but she heard the floor creak under him as he stepped out of its path.

"You can sleep when you're dead." He growled at her.

"Unless you've come to take me to the light, I'll sleep now." She pulled her comforter up over her head and snuggled deep into the bed, trying to ignore him. Her eyes were closed, but she knew he wasn't going to leave until he'd done what he came to do. She would do her best to ignore him until he forced the issue. Grabbing hold of the blanket, he pulled it off her from the bottom of the bed.

"Go away!" Jael shouted, glad she'd slept in a pair of shorts and tank top instead of just the T-shirt she was accustomed to. The shorts were small and tight, but at least all her important parts were covered.

"Come. I'll make the coffee."

Coffee was the only way he would get her out of bed. Jael let out a grumble as she crawled off the mattress. She fought the heaviness of sleep weighing down her eyelids. The clock on the bedside table glared at her in the dark room. Seven o'clock in the morning.

"Someone needs to explain to him the proper visiting times," she mumbled.

She continued complaining to herself about her mere hour of sleep when the floor-to-ceiling window curtains that spanned the front of her condo were opened.

Oh, he is going to pay now.

She'd spent good money to have dark, sun-blocking curtains made for such large windows. Though she loved her loft looking out over Crystal Falls without those curtains, she would have moved. Being a night owl through and through, she didn't want to be woken by the sun each morning.

With an open floor plan, the kitchen opening into the dining area, as well as the living room. The floor to ceiling windows lining the wall gave Jael full advantage of the scenic setting outside, at least when the expensive curtains were open.

"Are you crazy?" she yelled as she pounded down the wrought iron staircase that led to the loft bedroom.

She found him, all six-foot-five, clad in black from head to toe, at the bottom of the stairs with a coffee cup in his hand.

He eyed her, one eyebrow cocked, a smirk on his face. "I'm Death. Crazy is part of the job description."

Umm, coffee. Her mouth watered from the smell. Taking the mug from him, Jael enjoyed the aroma of rich, strong coffee. When the hot liquid touched her tongue, she forgot all about being mad.

"What do you want?" She eyed him over the rim of the cup.

"You have had enough time. It's time to take your place."

"Enough time!" She wanted to take his head off. *How could he think a month was enough time? Does this death guy not understand Mom and I were so close? I wonder if you can kill Death, or maybe get some charm or something to repel him? Would chalk around the windows and doors keep him away, like voodoo practitioners believe? I'll try just about anything.*

"Yes. Ann has been dead for over a month," Death said, casting her a look that implied she was overreacting.

"You think a month is enough time to get over the death of my mother?"

"There are souls who need your help," he stated matter-of-factly.

"I don't care. You think you can show up while my mother is on her deathbed and tell me it's my duty and I'll just do it? I have a job, I don't need another one. Not to mention I sure as heck don't need you hanging around like some demon."

He leaned against the back of her white sectional sofa, a complete contrast to his outfit. "It was a mistake for Ann not to tell you before. She should have prepared you."

"You're blaming my mother!" Unable to believe what she was hearing, she stared at him. He had a way of getting under her skin.

"I am only stating the truth."

This man had no respect for anyone's feelings. He just said what he felt and didn't worry if someone was hurt by it.

"Get out of my house!"

"Jael, you know that won't solve anything. We need each other. You can't get rid of me." He stepped toward her until he was right in front of her, and ran his finger down her cheek, sending mixed feelings through her body. She wanted to be revolted by his touch. Instead her body betrayed her, yearning for more.

"I don't need you." She sat the coffee mug on the end table, and walked to the steps.

"Jael, you will regret this. I have been protecting you, but I can do that no longer." With that, he disappeared.

"What's that supposed to mean? Protecting me how?"

Wow, that was easier than I thought.

She never would have guessed she would get rid of him, but now that he was gone, she missed him. She wanted to run her hands over his chest, her fingers through his black hair. She hated how her body betrayed her every time he was near. Her heart skipped a beat, her fingers itched to touch him, and her mouth went dry.

Oh, that man gets on my nerves, but what a body.

Exhausted, she climbed the steps. She was nearly at the top when her world crashed down around her. Pressure built in her chest, pressing against her lungs until she wasn't sure she'd be able to take another breath. Darkness faded in from the corners, threatening to engulf her.

A moan tore from her throat seconds before she collapsed on the landing.

"Death, what did you do?" She screamed as her breath returned, and pain ripped through her body.

"You called?" Death appeared. His black boots were the only thing she could see, her body hurt too much to look up.

"What did you do to me?"

"Unleashed your abilities. The pain you're experiencing is because your mother bound your powers. When she did it, she told me she would unleash them a little at a time, but it will pass in a few minutes. I had no choice but to undo it all at once, instead of slowly."

"No choice?" Her vision faded to gray, blue streaks throughout it.

"There's a situation that needs your attention, and you need your abilities to be able to perform your duty." He reached down, placed his hands under her arms and dragged her to her feet. The touch eased the fear, sending chills through her from his cool skin. Despite this, her legs wouldn't hold her. She would have fallen back to the floor if Death didn't keep his arm around her waist. "Let's get you to the bed."

She didn't understand what was happening but she sure as hell didn't like the pain tearing through her body. How was she supposed to do anything let alone help Death if she couldn't even see straight? The second his hand moved from her arm, the pain poured back into her.

"Undo this. Pain, it's too much." Feeling like she was dying, she laid back on the bed, letting her legs dangle over the side.

"It will be over soon." He wrapped his hand around hers.

"Why does that help?" Exhaustion pressed on her with such force she couldn't keep her eyes open.

"I have abilities to help you get the job done. This is one of mine but it will only work on you." She squeezed his hand, the pain turning to a burning sensation, making it feel like every nerve ending was on fire. "Take a few deep breaths, it's almost over."

With no other choice, she tried to breathe, to stop wiggling on the bed because every move made the agony worse. How did Death expect her to help him after this? The urge to rip his heart out, to make him suffer as she was, coursed through her until she was filled with rage.

As quickly as the pain started, it ended. Slowly her breathing became regular, and her heart no longer felt like it would explode under the pressure. The episode left her exhausted, her stomach still turning as an afterthought to the pain. Keeping her eyes shut, she pulled her hand from his.

"I told you I wanted nothing to do with this, and still you forced it on me?"

"You left me no choice, I need your help." He stood from the bed before she gathered the energy to kick him off. "Open your eyes and you'll see your destiny before you."

"This is wrong and you know it." She propped herself on her elbows, her eyes still closed. She was scared of what she might see when she opened them.

"No, what is wrong is what's happening in this world. The spirits need your help, you can't ignore your legacy any longer without consequences. Now open your eyes."

She ran her hand through her long blonde hair, and finally did what he asked. The world before her had a grayish overtone, streaks of blue mixed into the landscape. Blinking, she tried to right her vision. Nothing changed, no matter how many times she blinked.

Now that she was no longer in agony, he withdrew his hand and stood. The instant he was no longer touching her, she missed the contact. Ever since Death came into her life, she longed for physical contact with him despite the fact he only brought her misery.

"What the hell did you do to me?"

"We covered that." The concern was gone from his face, only to be replaced with the usual smirk.

"Well, take it back!" She scooted up on the bed, closer to the headboard, placing distance between them. "My mother might have accepted this curse, but everyone thought she was crazy. I won't have that. I already have a job. I'm a paramedic. If I go around talking to people no one else can see, they'll lock me up."

The hints of silver from his sapphire eyes sparkled in the light. "This is something you'll have to learn to work into your life."

"I'm supposed to save people from death, not help them find it!"

He turned so his hip was against the bedpost and watched her. "Would you curse these people to a life of misery and wandering the earth lost?"

Damn him. She became a paramedic to save people, she couldn't leave someone suffering in limbo, wandering the earth alone if she could help it. She was too softhearted for that. Not sure who she was more angry with, Death or herself, it was too much for her brain to comprehend. Especially without more coffee.

"I didn't think so." His lips curled up into a smile that made his eyes sparkle. "Now I suggest you get dressed, they'll be arriving any moment."

"They?"

"Those needing your help. To a spirit you are like a giant lighthouse, they can see you no matter where you are. When they're ready, they will come to you. Now dress, there's more coffee downstairs. Trust me, you'll need it." He left her more confused than before.

"Wait, what about my vision?" She called after him.

Without turning around, he paused at the top of the steps, his hand resting on the wrought iron banister. "You'll get used to it. You're seeing Thanatos, it's the plane where the spirits exist. There they can move between places faster, they don't have to worry about walking through people. That tends to cause a chill to even the non-sensitive, and is extremely uncomfortable for anyone the least bit sensitive to the supernatural. With time you'll be able to build shields to help you block it. One thing at a time. First you need to be made aware of the situation at hand." With that he continued down the steps.

Situation? She wanted to ask about it but if spirits were on their way, she needed to dress. Sliding off the bed she expected the blue streaks to stay where they were, but they moved with her, keeping their distance. What where those streaks? What happened if she touched one? Most importantly, how did she know Thanatos was the Greek word for death? She'd never read about it, and never seen the word anywhere before.

Downstairs, she found Death leaning against the back of her sofa, another mug of coffee in his hand. For a brief moment she wondered how he knew she needed her daily dose of coffee to get started. Coffee was her lifeblood, without it she couldn't get by.

He handed it to her, taking in her choice of outfit with a smile.

"What?" She looked down at her hip hugging stonewashed blue jeans, and gray off the shoulder sweater. It looked fine when she was upstairs, so why was he watching her with amusement?

"I'm only amazed by the transformation in less than five minutes. I've known women in the past that couldn't look that good after hours of preparation."

His words sent her heart fluttering. Had he just hit on her? She wasn't sure and before she could question it his smile disappeared. Everything turned serious in an instant.

"They are nearing." He pushed off the back of the sofa and came to stand in front of her. "Spirits are the same as they were in life, some are easy to deal with while others are more difficult. What you need to make them understand is you're in charge. Don't let them walk all over you. Due to the situation, it's likely they'll be upset, but I'm here with you to help in any way you need me to. Most importantly, they can't hurt you. Spirits can't even touch this plane unless you bring them over, even then they are completely under your control."

Nervousness wracked her body, her hand shook so much she nearly spilled the coffee. "I don't know what you want me to do. Bring them over how?"

He reached out, taking the coffee from her and placing it on the end table before taking both of her hands in his. "Normally we'd start slow, letting you learn as you went, but with the situation we don't have that luxury. You're about to get thrown into it head first, but I'll be with you. It's going to be okay."

"Situation? Are you going to explain that or just leave me in the dark?"

"There is a serial killer in Crystal Falls."

Chapter Two

Jael's eyes grew wide with shock. *A serial killer.* Cleg never said anything about a serial killer, and as one of two detectives Crystal Falls Police Department had on their payroll, he would have known. It was unlike her brother to keep her in the dark about something so menacing. As a paramedic, she was at risk with each call. First responders were normally notified if something dangerous was lurking in the shadows of Crystal Falls, so they could watch their backs.

A woman no older than twenty with long blonde hair, two light pink streaks on each side of her face, appeared before her. Dressed in tight straight leg jeans, a black sweater, and knee high heeled boots. Besides the fact she'd just walked through a wall, the woman was transparent.

"You ready?" Death whispered, giving her hands a quick squeeze before letting go of them to stand next to her.

All concept of words were gone, and the reality of the situation at hand sank in quickly. Being the Grim Reaper was going to take its toll on her life quickly if spirits could just show up out of the blue, walking through walls whenever they pleased.

"This can't be happening," Jael whispered.

"It's true then. Maria said if I found the light they'd help me. You can see me, can't you?"

Jael wasn't sure why but she expected the spirit's voice to be distant and ghostly. It was nothing like that. She sounded like a flesh and blood person.

Jael shook her head. "I can't do this. You have the wrong person."

"I don't have the wrong person. Maria has been around a long time. She told me the light would be the Grim Reaper. That's you. You have to help me. If you don't, then I won't cross over."

"I'm not the light. I'm just a person. There is nothing I can do for you," Jael said, holding up her hands in a gesture of helplessness.

"You have to help me, or I can't leave." The spirit stepped forward, making Jael want to retreat. It was eerie that the woman's footsteps didn't make a sound, not even the click of heels against the hardwood floor.

"I don't know *how* to help you. This isn't my job, I'm a paramedic. Who is Maria?"

"Another spirit, she has been here a while and doesn't want to cross over and leave her children. She knows a lot and helped me adjust when I first died."

Even with the proof staring her in the face, Jael didn't want to believe this was actually happening. "I still say you have the wrong person." She crossed her arms under her breasts and fought the shiver creeping up her spine.

"Hello, lady. I'm a freaking ghost." The spirit wiggled her fingers in sarcastic greeting. "You can see me; no one else can. How can I be kidding about this?"

"I don't know."

"You don't know? What kind of Grim Reaper are you?" The spirit raised her hands and threw her head back as though seeking an answer from the ceiling. Jael imagined the woman rolling her eyes in frustration.

She could hear the anger in the ghost's voice. "This is all new to me."

That stopped the ghost in her tracks. "Are you freaking telling me this is your first rodeo? Of all the people in the world, I get the green Grim Reaper!"

"It's not like I wanted to be the Grim Reaper." Jael turned to Death who remained quiet through the whole conversation. He hadn't even moved from her side. "If I'm going to deal with this crap, I need more coffee." She didn't bother keeping the petulance from her tone. People were waking her up and pestering her left and right. Jael wanted nothing more than to sleep in peace.

"Maddie, this is her first assignment. The passing of the former Grim Reaper was unfortunate and threw Jael into this headfirst," Death explained to the spirit.

"Unfortunate? What is unfortunate is the fact I was murdered! He is going to do it again unless she stops him. We don't have time for her to pussyfoot around, or doubt what she is." Maddie placed her hands on her hips and glared at them.

Jael turned to Death, eyeing him. "I need to speak with you, *now*." She stormed off to the kitchen. Being open to the rest of the condo, it would provide no privacy from the spirit, but it was the best she could do unless she wanted to be forced out of her own home.

"Give us a moment," Death told Maddie before following Jael.

Jael poured more coffee into the mug and brought it close to her face before Death caught up with her. She inhaled deeply, breathing in the spicy aroma. "I know you said this is my legacy but I just can't. I don't know how to help her. You need to find someone else."

"There is no one else. Maddie and the others need your help and you can do this." He leaned against the kitchen bar, his elbow resting on the granite counter. "If you'll trust me I'll see you get through this. With a little time it will become second nature to you. Your body is still trying to adjust to the new abilities, and this is all a lot to take in but it's your destiny. One I know you'll excel at."

She took a sip of her coffee, letting it calm her from the inside out. "I don't know how to help her. I'm not a police officer, I can't go chasing down a serial killer."

"No, but you can pass on the information from her and the others to Cleg or whoever is working the case. That will be the key to catching the bastard, and the spirits can cross."

"How am I supposed to explain that to Cleg?" Her twin brother was too scientific. Without proof, he'd never believe her.

"You'll be surprised by him." Once again he gave her a smirk that let her know he was still hiding something. "Let's talk to Maddie, gather whatever information she can give us, and then we'll deal with Cleg."

"Surprised by him, how?"

He gave her a quick wink. "That's his to tell. Come, Maddie is waiting."

She let out a string of curses as he walked away from her. It was becoming tiresome to be kept in the dark. When did her world become so full of secrets? It had been turned upside down since her mother's passing, and became worse in the last few hours.

Placing her mug on the counter, she took a deep breath and went to meet her destiny head first. "Maddie, you said you were murdered, did you see who?"

"I saw him as he sliced my skin into ribbons before…cutting my throat." Maddie's transparent figure shivered as if she was cold. Could spirits feel cold?

"If he cut you, how come I don't see any damage?" A hint of doubt crept into Jael's voice.

Death, who was a step behind her, cleared his throat. "It depends on the spirits. If they are strong enough they can choose to appear as they were before their death, hiding their wounds. Otherwise, they will appear as they died. Clothes, attitude, and everything else will be the same no matter which they choose. The only difference is they can make themselves more presentable."

Jael nodded, and for the first time actually studied the spirit before her. It was surprising how closely Maddie resembled Jael, almost as if she were looking into a mirror. They both had the same creamy completion and blonde hair. Each stood five-foot-five, with the same athletic build. It was unnerving, especially when another woman appeared behind Maddie with very similar looks.

"When you didn't come back, we thought she blasted you to oblivion." The new spirit eyed Maddie with admiration.

"Everything is fine, Christy. Go back to the others and let them know I'll come once I bring the Grim Reaper up to speed on our situation."

Maddie's words sent Christy back from wherever she'd come. One minute Christy was there and the next she'd walked through the wall and was gone. Jael couldn't get over how they could do that. Being on the fifth floor of the building, Jael wondered what happened when the spirit was on the other side of the wall. Did they fall to the ground? Could they fly?

"Thanatos is different than this plane. Building floors don't affect them as they do for you. In time you'll understand." Death explained as if she had stated her questions aloud.

"Can we get back to what happened to me and the others?" Maddie's impatience was clear in her voice.

Jael nodded. "Tell me what happened."

"I was passing through on my way back to Billings from vacation. It was late, after one in the morning, but I wanted to get back home to my own bed. My car broke down just outside the town limits, and I was waiting for a tow when I must have dozed off." Maddie paused, crossing her arms over her chest as if she was cold. "I woke to my window being smashed in. He pulled me through, and when I fought back he pulled out a syringe and injected me."

"What did the injection do? Were you conscious?" Jael knew if Maddie had been awake she might have seen her attacker, but to be awake during such an ordeal in the final minutes of her life had to be pure hell.

"I don't know what it was but I couldn't move. I was awake through the whole thing."

"It had to be some type of neuromuscular blocking drug," Death explained. "You'd have seen and felt everything but would have been unable to fight back."

"All I know is that after I was drugged, I couldn't even scream. He sliced tiny ribbons of my skin off, kept adding them to a plastic container like he planned to keep it. It seemed like I laid there on the hood of my car for hours as he dragged it out. Then he leaned close, pressing his lips to my ear, and whispered, *that's all that's valuable from you.* His voice was thick, and he had a southern accent. He cut my throat and left me to die."

A chill coursed through Jael at the thought of being skinned alive before finally being killed. The chill seemed to sink into her bones, stealing all the warmth from her soul. Jael was impressed with how normal Maddie seemed, and she couldn't help but wonder why.

"I'm new to this, but you seem too calm."

"I was the first…victim." Maddie clenched her fists. "The others needed me to be in control, so I had no choice but to get over what happened. The others aren't so lucky. The latest victim is the worst. It's why I've come to you first, to prepare you."

Jael took a moment to let that sink in. It seemed reasonable enough, but it also made her fearful of what the others were going to be like when she questioned them. "Why would he collect the skin? Did he do it to the others as well?"

Maddie gave a slow nodded. "All of us have skin missing from different areas of our body. It's like he's putting it together, a complete body of skin."

The thought a serial killer collecting skin in her hometown made Jael sick. "If you saw him again, would you recognize him? Tell me anything you can remember about him."

Maddie didn't answer. She walked around the sofa and sank down. Up until that point Jael stood near the steps not wanting to sit when she thought the spirit wouldn't be able to. Jael followed, snatching the red crochet blanket from the back of the sofa before sitting across from Maddie.

"He seemed like he fit in, there was nothing out of the ordinary about him, but I could never get rid of the memory of his face. He seemed so ordinary, the cowboy hat and boots, he looked like he had worked on a ranch all day. I could see dark brown or black hair sticking out from under the cowboy hat, and he was over six feet tall and muscular. Well, he'd have to be, to be able to lift me out of the car through the window. He was tanned, and there was a long scar going from his earlobe that disappeared under his shirt."

"How many victims are there so far?" Jael asked.

"Including me, four. Shelly was just after me, and two others. I had Shelly stay with the others who were too scared to leave Thanatos, with the promise I'd scope out the Reaper and return to them."

"I'll need to speak with them as well if I'm going to…" Jael's words faded. What was she going to do? She couldn't hunt this murderer herself, and she wasn't sure Cleg was going to believe her.

Death stepped forward, placing his hand on Jael's shoulder. "It needs to be one at a time so that the information isn't tainted by another's tale."

Maddie looked from Jael to Death before settling on Jael. "Shelly is eager to speak with you, the others are fearful they will be destroyed. Another spirit has put fear into them, telling horror stories that they will be blasted to oblivion, or worse…that the Reaper will leave them to rot in Thanatos."

"I'll help you, whatever it takes. I'll make sure you can cross over." Jael reassured Maddie as well as herself. In that moment it finally became clear why her mother put up with the ability, the crazy looks from others, not to mention the spirits. Like her mother, Jael wouldn't be able to turn her back on those in need, even if they were already dead.

When Jael finished speaking with each of the victims, she was exhausted and depressed. There was a serial killer stalking her town, more importantly a certain type of woman. Jael fit the profile.

She rose from the chair and stepped toward the counter. She needed another mug of piping hot coffee before calling her brother.

"Shouldn't you call Cleg?" Death leaned against the kitchen counter looking delicious as usual.

She forced her gaze back to pouring the coffee and away from picturing him naked. Her cheeks heated with embarrassment. What had gotten into her? "I need a little more coffee, and then I will."

"A little more? Woman, you've drank nearly half the pot in twenty minutes. You should be able to run a marathon by now. I think you're putting it off, *kochanie*."

My darling?

"I didn't know you spoke Polish. Hell, I don't speak Polish."

"Like you, I speak every language. You recognize the translation?" He was obviously testing her translation skills.

"Yes, it means my darling."

He nodded. "*Kochanie*, you're delaying."

Plopping down on the bar stool, her coffee mug in hand, she stared at him. "Delaying…you could say that. What the hell am I supposed to tell Cleg?"

"Nothing over the phone. What needs to be said between the two of you should be done in person." He nodded at her cell phone on the counter. "Now call him."

With a heavy lump in her stomach, she leaned forward, her fingers closing around the cell phone. Now or never, oh how she wished it could be never. Her thumb slid across the screen, unlocking the phone and pulling up her contacts. Throwing caution to the wind, she called Cleg.

"Jael, this isn't a good time, I'm working on a case." The tiredness was clear in his voice.

"A case of a series of murders of woman in their twenties, blonde hair…"

"How do you know anything of it?" All of a sudden he sounded alert.

"Are you confirming it then?" Cleg's silence answered her question. "Can you get away for a bit? Then I'll explain."

Papers shuffled as if he was trying to find something. "If you can feed your dear brother, I'll slip away in about twenty minutes, but you have some *serious* explaining to do."

"I'll see you then." Ending the call, she glanced up at Death. "He'll be here in twenty minutes."

"Then I will go, call if you need anything."

"Call? I don't have your number." She started to hand him the cell phone so he could add it.

He waved it away. "We're connected, and when you think of me I'll appear. It's a safety measure in case you're ever in a situation where you can't call for me, but need me."

She didn't like the sound of the implication. "Why would I ever be in a situation where safety is an issue? I'm a paramedic."

"It's a precaution, nothing more."

A sudden impression there was more to it than just a precaution lingered in her stomach. Being the Grim Reaper would bring danger to her doorsteps occasionally, maybe more than occasionally. This was her first assignment and she was already thrown neck deep in danger.

"Jael." Death's voice pulled her from her thoughts seconds before he clasped his hand over hers. "Be straight forward with Cleg. He'll understand, and has something to get off his chest as well."

Chapter Three

Setting the sandwich with a side of pasta salad in front of Cleg, Jael noticed the dark circles under his eyes. How long had it been since he'd had a good night's sleep, or a hot meal? If she knew things were this bad, she'd have fixed him something better than a cold sandwich.

"Why are you looking at me like that?"

"I was wondering how long you've been working this case. The dark circles are screaming you haven't slept in days, and the way your eyes glazed over I'm wondering when you had something that wasn't out of the precinct vending machine."

He didn't dispute her words, instead he grabbed part of the sandwich. "Little sister, I believe you are stalling. How did you know of the murders?"

"Ahhh." She leaned against the counter. "This is going to sound insane, but I've seen the women that have been killed."

"You've come into your abilities then." He took a bite of the sandwich and watched her.

Her knees went weak. "You knew? How?"

"Mom sheltered you, she didn't want to have to deal with it until you had to, but yes I knew. I have an ability of my own that I've kept hidden." Cleg polished off the rest of the sandwich before rising. "Jael, you need to sit for this story."

She followed Cleg to the sofa on weak knees, anxious to get the whole thing over. The air chilled around her, forcing a shiver. Sinking down onto the sofa she pulled the crochet blanket around her shoulders.

He sat down at the end of the sofa. "Mom always tried to shelter us from the supernatural, to protect us from the decisions she made. During puberty, my powers formed and she could no longer hide the truth from me. I'm basically a human lie detector, it's helped me get where I am. I can also force people to tell me what I need to know. When I went to mom about it, she tried to tell me I was just more in tune with people. I knew she lied. That's when everything came out. Jael, I know you're the Grim Reaper."

She wasn't surprised by his ability. After all, she knew it was impossible to lie to him. "Why didn't you tell me?"

"Mom asked me not to. She did it to protect you. After she passed, I knew *he'd* come to you. I knew when you were ready you'd tell me, then I could tell you the whole story."

"He? The whole story, there's more?"

"He as in Death. Knowing mom died without unleashing your powers, she'd left it to Death to do it." Cleg shook his head, as if unable to believe their mother would do it. "As for the whole story, yes there's more. Haven't you ever wondered who our father was? You get your abilities from Mom's side, but mine are not from her."

Over the years, Jael had wondered who her father was. It was one of the only sore spots between her and her mom. "I asked her years ago but she wouldn't tell me. Does this mean our father is like Mom was too?"

Cleg looked away from her, as if he worried how she would take what he was about to say. "Mom didn't tell you because she feared you'd think less of her. She was young, in college for her nursing degree, when she met a man who she thought could give her the world. He was handsome and treated her like a queen, everything she always hoped for. In the end he lied to her about who and what he really was, and by the time she found out she was already pregnant with us."

"Who was he? Have you met him?"

"I haven't met him in person, I've only spoke to him on the phone once. He is Lucifer, the Devil."

The Devil? Cleg had to be joking. Shock, anger and more emotions than she could name passed through her like a speeding bullet. How could they be the children of the Prince of Darkness? She always believed it was a myth to keep everyone on the right track or fear going to Hell. Now she felt uncertain and off balance. One day she was the daughter of an average single mother, a paramedic, and now her whole life had been flipped upside down. How was she supposed to put the pieces together again and move past all of this? Where there more surprises lurking in the dark? What else wasn't

Cleg and Death telling her? She wasn't a little naïve girl that had to be sheltered. If this was supposed to be her life, she had a right to know everything.

"Jael…" Cleg knelt in front of her, shaking her shoulders until she glanced up at him. "Are you listening to me?"

She blinked, pushing away the cobwebs. Completely lost in thought, she hadn't even noticed Cleg had moved. "What?"

"I've never seen you like this, are you okay?"

"Okay?" Shaking her head, she met his gaze with wide eyes and a touch of anger. "No, I'm not okay. How the hell will things ever be okay again? I am the daughter of the freaking Devil!"

With a cool breeze, Death appeared before her looking slightly amused. For once she welcomed the visit. Maybe he could shine more light on the whole barbaric situation. "Well, I see you're handling this well."

"Why was everyone keeping secrets from me? Damn it, I hate being kept in the dark, but more importantly it's my life and I had a right to know!"

Death's appearance made her forget that others couldn't see him, so to Cleg she most likely looked like she was screaming at thin air. Cleg probably thought she had cracked like their mother, but what she had to say to Death couldn't wait.

Death held his hand out as if to say *don't blame me*. "It wasn't my place to tell the story, it was your mother's."

"He's right, it was Mom's story to tell," Cleg added.

Cleg coming to Death's rescue wasn't the only thing that confused her. "You can see him? Wait…why can you see him but no one else can? I looked like I complete lunatic when I asked the nurse to remove him from Mom's hospital room. She couldn't see him, and thought I was insane."

"Unless I choose to appear among them, humans can't see me. If you remember correctly, my words were, *I wouldn't recommend that,* when you threatened to call security," Death explained.

"Then why can Cleg see you?"

"I see him because of our heritage." Cleg stood and walked to the windows. "Jael, I'm the heir to our father's throne."

The air was forced from her lungs. She felt lightheaded as if she had left her body and was watching everything through someone else. Her body forgot how to function, to breathe. "What?" It came out more of a whisper than she planned.

Her twin brother stood by the windows, the sun making his blond hair look golden. He looked like an angel, authority pouring off him. It wasn't just because he was the top detective of Crystal Falls Police. She couldn't believe he was the heir to Hell.

"It's not like I wanted this. Just as you've been dropped in your destiny, it seems as though I've been too." Cleg didn't turn to look at her.

"When I help spirits cross over, where are they going? Am I cursing them to Hell?"

"I swear you're not." Death held up one hand, palm facing her, as if pledging the truth. "If they're meant to go to Hell, they would go immediately. There would be nothing holding them back. Spirits don't get a chance to take care of unfinished business when they're going to Hell."

"Then how…"

Death came and sat next to her, taking her hand in his. "*Kochanie,* you and Cleg are like two sides of one coin. You could say the good and bad of the world. Cleg has a choice to take his place as heir or not, and if he embraces his destiny he has the choice as to what to do with Hell. When the two of you were born, your destinies where divided between both of you. It's a forewarning on what will happen, but only the two of you can make the choices."

"What choices?"

Death's thumb teased along her knuckles in a comforting yet somewhat intimate way. "This is not the time. Right now you need time to digest this, and there are spirits that need you."

"You're right. Maddie and the others need me to focus, but I have one question." Jael looked to Cleg. "Did Mom know who she slept with when she conceived us?"

Cleg turned from the window and nodded. "She knew and didn't care, she loved our father. It wasn't until after she was pregnant that she realized the danger. I don't believe she ever stopped loving him, instead she put our safety in front of her own feelings. Our father's enemies are numerous and dangerous. If they find out we live, they will hunt us down like prey."

"Now that you're both aware of your destiny and Jael's abilities have been unleashed, you will come into additional powers," Death said. "Ones that will keep you safe from your opposition, safer if you choose to work together instead of against each other."

Jael turned to Death. "I can't turn my back on Cleg."

"As I said, those are things only the two of you can decide. Whatever path the two of you choose, I will be by your side, *kochanie*." Death brought her hand to his lips and kissed it gently.

"Jael, I don't think you understand if I can't fight my destiny I will be a threat to you."

She turned her head to look at him with such speed she might've been possessed. Twins against each other. Was that truly what her destiny might hold? Looking at Cleg, she doubted she'd live through it. There was little chance she could actually turn her back on him, and less of a chance she could go up against him. There was something about the way Death spoke that made her think if Cleg chose to embrace his dark side that it would be up to her to kill him. She couldn't do that. He was her twin, part of her.

"Cleg, you're not evil. I know you'll do what is right. Look at you, you're a cop for heaven's sake, you fight evil, you don't join it."

She wanted to go to him but something held her back. There was a tiny seed of doubt deep within her that she didn't want to admit to. Death had already proved to her that it was nearly impossible to turn away from destiny, and she didn't know what the Prince of Darkness was offering Cleg to sway him.

"As you my sister are a paramedic, you're supposed to save people from death not help them find it." Cleg dragged his hand through his short hair. "There's nothing fair about any of this, so let's just forget it for now."

"Very well." She was thankful to move on to something else. She needed time to let everything she'd learned sink in before she could make any decisions about her future. "Can you confirm there's a serial killer then?"

"Yes." Cleg nodded, pulling his phone from his pocket. "It was only confirmed this morning when the third victim was found. The media has not picked up on any of this yet but it's only a matter of time. You mentioned Maddie, I'm assuming you're referring to Madeline Darcy. She was the first victim and was found three days ago."

Only three? The police were missing one of the bodies, since Jael knew of four victims. "Maddie has two pink highlights around her face," Jael told him, wanting confirmation they were talking about the same person.

"Here." Cleg walked toward her and held out his phone.

She slipped her hand from Death's and took the phone. A morgue picture of Maddie filled the screen. Maddie looked so much younger, her skin pasty white.

"That's her." Even seeing Maddie as a transparent figure moving around the condo hadn't drove it home that the girl was truly dead, but the picture of her on the stainless steel table did.

"Scroll over and verify the other two."

Her finger slid over the screen, bringing up similar pictures of Shelly and Jamie.

"You're missing Annabell."

Cleg shook his head. "There's only three women and I hope to keep it that way."

"Annabell was killed last night off Johnsonville Road. Have you figured out why he's skinning them alive? Any clues as to why he's keeping the skin?"

"For each woman it's a different part skinned. On Maddie it was her stomach, Shelly her left thigh, and Jamie the right thigh. The department's shrink believes he's eating it." Cleg shuttered. "The M.E. has discovered there've been bites taken out of each of the women. What no one can figure out yet is why there's no defensive wounds on any of the victims. It's the missing piece of the puzzle since the autopsy shows their throats were slit after he skinned them."

"He used a neuromuscular blocking drug," Death explained. "I believe it might be vecuronium. If he didn't slit their throats they would have died anyway, vecuronium would have paralyzed the diaphragm making it impossible to breathe."

Jael's stomach churned with the thoughts of their last minutes alive. It had to be horrific, and they were stuck in limbo until the bastard was caught. It was her job to help them find peace.

Cleg was facing them, but he seemed to be looking through them, staring off into his thoughts. "I'll have the M.E. check the blood work. If that's what he used, it would show up since they died before it could be processed through the system. It might also make him traceable. The people with access to it would be limited."

"Neurologists and pharmacists would be the likely choices. Registered nurses, doctors are also possible. Still it would narrow the search considerably." Jael paused, wondering how long it would take to run through the possibilities. In Crystal Falls, there couldn't be that many, but surrounding towns, especially Billings, would add to the possibilities. "Travis might be able to find out at the hospital if any vecuronium has gone missing without raising any alarm bells."

She'd dated Doctor Travis Smith for a short period after his divorce, and they had remained close friends when they agreed their relationship wasn't working. He was still in love with his ex-wife; the only reason they'd split was his job as the emergency room doctor required long hours, and Peg was tired of playing second fiddle to his career.

"Let's not explore that option yet. I'll check with the M.E., but first I need to find Annabell's body." Cleg took his phone back from her and clipped it onto his belt. His expression was somber, and it was clear he was wishing he'd stopped the killer before the fourth woman had met her end. "Did any of the women get a good look at their killer?"

Jael nodded. "They were all able to give a good description. I spoke with them separately so their stories wouldn't be influenced. I can tell you what he looked like, but how's that going to help you?"

"Actually, the Captain might approve you sitting with our sketch artist. It would require a little explanation, but it could save lives. He's a hellhound, so he'll understand our interesting situation. I've got to go, but I'll let you know what I find." Cleg eyed Death for a moment, and there was a touch of hostility in his gaze. "Keep her safe."

Death nodded. "Always."

Jael rose form the sofa, drawing Cleg's attention. "I can take care of myself."

"My dear sister, I never doubt you there, I only meant you fit the type of woman the killer is looking for. Stay out of danger. I'll be in touch soon." Cleg strolled toward the door when she called out to him.

"There's another thing, I think he might be targeting women who have broken down. Both Maddie and Shelly were traveling through. They stopped at a rest stop just before hitting Johnsonville Road. It's possible he's doing something to the cars."

"I'll check into that." He called to her seconds before he opened the front door, and disappeared leaving her alone with Death.

Chapter Four

"What am I supposed to do now? I can't just sit here knowing those women are waiting for justice, or Heaven forbid he's out there stalking another woman." Jael paced, unable to stay still. With Jamie and Annabell feeling safer in Thanatos, the spirits weren't looming about waiting, but she knew they were just as anxious about getting it over with as she was.

"*Kochanie*, he's right, you are the killer's type. You go chasing after him, and you are putting yourself in danger. You've done what you could for the moment, now let Cleg handle it." Death sat on the sofa, his gaze following her as she paced.

She stopped in front of the sofa. "Why do you call me *kochanie?*"

"Because that's what you are to me." He explained it as if it was obvious.

"When mom passed, she said the Grim Reaper is the first daughter of each generation. I'm to pass this on to my child. That's why we could never be."

"We could if you gave us a chance. There's no reason you couldn't swell with child and carry your legacy on. Is that why you're pushing me away?" He raised an eyebrow at her.

"You're *dead*, that is the reason I couldn't have your child."

Death let out a lighthearted chuckle. "Dead? What gave you that impression?"

"I don't know, maybe the fact no one else can see you?"

"Cleg can see me." He glided toward her until he stood in front of her.

"That's because he's the heir to Hell's throne. If no one can see you that means you're not human. I can't be with someone who can't be there when I need him."

"I'm always there for you. All you have to do is call me." She turned around when he paused.

Debate crossed his strong features. She wanted to say something, but his eyes held hers, causing her voice to fail her. He reached for her hand. "Jael, I'm not dead nor have I ever been born. I'm a thought brought into creation. I can make people see me if I want, there just never seems to be a reason."

"A thought?"

"Yes, a thought. There was a need for someone to teach each Grim Reaper their job, to oversee the dead as they find their way to the light, and to make sure those who don't deserve the light never find it."

She tried to wrap her mind around his explanation, but at that moment rational thoughts were beyond her. Maybe, once she had more sleep, she'd consider his words again.

As if summoned by her need to do something her cell phone rang. She snatched it off the sofa cushion, slid her finger over the screen and hit speakerphone. There was only one person who had that ringtone, her paramedic partner.

"Hello, Nathan."

"The Lieutenant needs us to cover a shift. There was a riot last night, two of the paramedics on duty were injured. Paul is home with a concussion, his partner's in the hospital."

Sinking down onto the sofa, she leaned her head back and closed her eyes, listening to Nathan's husky voice. Since Nathan transferred from the fire department to the ambulance squad, she wanted more than just friendship with him. His deeply muscled body, sandy brown hair, and green eyes haunted her dreams. Nathan was a natural flirt, any interest he had showed never seemed to convince her that anything could be between them. She stood by waiting, doing her best to be content with their friendship. Now she was trapped between two men she couldn't have.

"I have something going on." Not wanting to explain what she was busy with, she quickly added, "When do I need to be there?"

"We have an hour before the shift starts. Do you want me to pick you up?"

"Sure. I'll be ready." Ending the conversation, she turned back to Death. "At least work will keep my mind off of this."

Death smirked at her. "I will be going with you to watch over you."

"I can do my job without a bodyguard. I was a paramedic first, I can't give that up." She eyed him, anger teasing along the surface.

He raised his hand in front of him. "I said nothing about your profession. I only want to make sure you're safe."

Safe. She wasn't sure if she should be touched by his desire to protect her or insulted he thought she couldn't protect herself. In the end she decided on touched, after all there was a serial killer stalking her town.

Jael had just changed into her uniform and was coming down the stairs from the loft when her doorbell rang. "Please let there be no deaths on the job tonight." She mumbled to herself as she went for the door.

Opening it, she found Nathan looking as attractive as ever. His dark blue uniform fit snugly over his muscled body, earned from long hours in the gym. His shaggy sandy brown hair and piercing green eyes made him look more like a surfer than a paramedic. Heat raced through her body just from looking at him.

"Come in. I just need to grab my keys."

Strolling back toward the kitchen where her keys hung, she found Death waiting next to the bar. How she was supposed to get through the night without talking to Death, in turn making herself look like an idiot talking to thin air, she didn't know.

"What are you doing here?" Nathan asked.

"Nathan?" Jael asked, glancing from him to Death.

"He can see me," Death explained.

Her heart skipped a beat. Was Death making himself visible on purpose? Explaining Death as a ride along without prior permission was going to be difficult if not impossible. "How?"

"He's fae."

"What the hell is going on here?" Nathan asked, his gaze traveling between the two of them.

This night just got a hell of a lot harder. Jael wanted to curse her luck.

"Nathan, don't you think you should tell her now?" Death's voice was hard, but nowhere near as deadly as his stare.

"Leave us. I'll tell her."

"What are you two talking about?" Jael felt as if she'd missed something important.

Death moved across the room, giving them some privacy, the tension heavy in the air. "What was he talking about?" Jael stood to face Nathan.

Nathan stepped farther into the kitchen, avoiding her eyes. "With *his* presence here it's clear you're the Śmierć."

"What?" Jael didn't know what a Śmierć was and she didn't understand what that had to do with anything.

"It's the Polish version of the Grim Reaper," Nathan explained. "I can see him because my father was different. It was passed down to me, somewhat like your gift was passed from your mother."

"What do you mean? You can see spirits, too?"

"No. But I have my own gift." He paused as if he weren't sure how to continue. "As Death said, I'm fae, my gift is to heal. It's why I became a paramedic."

Jael stood there listening to him, but she wasn't sure what to say. She didn't doubt Nathan. After all, if she could see ghosts, why couldn't he heal someone? A few weeks ago she didn't believe any of this existed but now anything was possible.

"Let me show you." He took her hand, wrapping his over it. She had a cut on her hand, slicing deep through the soft skin between her thumb and index finger from a few days ago, when Death showed up while she was cooking, causing her to cut her finger instead of the potato. A warm glowing sensation surrounded her hand. It didn't hurt, but made her gasp in surprise.

When he let go, her hand was healed. There wasn't even a scar, no sign of the wound at all.

"Now, why couldn't I get that?" she asked, awed.

He let her hand fall away. "It's not as wonderful as it seems. It takes a lot out of you, and you should have seen it when I was a teenager and came into the gift. I couldn't control it and made a freak out of myself more than once."

"Have you ever used this on a call?"

"Last month. Remember the little girl who nearly drowned?"

"You saved her?" Memories from calls where mysteriously the patient recovered flooded back to her.

"Yeah. She was so young. If I couldn't save a little girl like that, then what use is my gift?"

She didn't know what to say. Forfeiting speech altogether, she nodded knowing she would have felt the same way. The deaths of children were one of the hardest parts of her job.

"Tonight's shift hasn't been too bad for a Friday night." Nathan leaned back in the booth they normally sat in at Dolly's Diner. On coffee breaks, they always stopped by Dolly's. They were regulars along with a lot of the other paramedics, firefighters, and the police department. Dolly treated them well and didn't mind them hanging out. When they stopped for food, she did her best to get it out right away in case they received a call.

A couple police officers walked in, discussing the riot from the night before. They nodded, sharing a friendly hello. The fire and police departments were across the street from each other, both having BBQs, picnics, parties, and other events together. Interfacing and getting along well.

"Have a care, Nat. We still have two hours. Don't say things like that until we park in the bay at the house and the locker room is in sight." Last week was the first week since she'd started back full time since her mother's death. Before that, it was part time while she dealt with all the arrangements, cleaning out her mother's house to rent out or sell. Adjusting back to full time had played havoc on her sleep schedule and it didn't help Death had interrupted her.

Death's presence in the ambulance had made the small space tense. Even now he sat next to her silently scanning the diner. What was the reason for the hostility between them? She made a mental note to ask Death about it once they were alone.

"You're too superstitious. Get over it. Tonight is going to be quiet. I know you want excitement, but not tonight," Nathan teased.

Jael rolled her eyes and lifted her coffee cup to signal to Dolly that she needed more. Suddenly, the quiet night ended with the radio cracking to life.

"ER seven. Johnsonville Road, mile marker thirty-seven. Code thirty-two, major trauma."

"On our way," Nathan said into the radio before reaching down to take a last gulp of coffee.

Jael threw money on the table while giving him a look that could kill. "This is all your fault."

"Blame me if you want, but it's not going to change the situation. We gotta roll with the flow, sweetie. I'll even buy breakfast when this is all said and done to make it up to you. Now get your butt in gear."

"Thanks, Dolly," they hollered, heading out the door.

Nathan slid the ambulance into drive, light and sirens blaring as they headed toward the scene.

"Johnsonville Road," Jael muttered.

"What is it?" Nathan asked as they sped along, rushing toward the call.

"She's not dead yet or she would have come to you." Death laid his hand on her shoulder.

"What the hell are you two talking about? We don't know anyone is dying." Nathan didn't look away from the road but his forehead was furrowed in confusion.

"It's a long story but there's a serial killer on the loose. I think he's favoring Johnsonville Road because of how quiet it is in the middle of the night." Jael looked to Death, the first trembles of fear showing. Fear of what she'd find when they arrived at the scene. Fear that the killer could be lurking nearby and see her.

"He's targeting attractive blonde women in their twenties, it's why I've accompanied Jael this night," Death explained, turning sideways in the jump seat in the patient area to look at her.

Nathan shot a quick glance at her. "You didn't think this was worth mentioning? As a first responder you could be placing yourself in more danger."

"I know, and it's part of the job. I will be fine. Cleg is working the case, so knowing my brother, the perp will be caught quickly." Jael tried to reassume Nathan as well as herself.

As they neared the scene, flashing lights lit the night sky like fireworks on the fourth of July. Police, fire, and now paramedics lined the side of the road. Nathan steered the ambulance at an angle behind the fire truck, leaving enough room they could do a quick three point turn to rush the patient back to Crystal Falls Hospital. Cleg's white police issued SUV stood out amongst all the marked cars just ahead.

Jael turned in her seat to look at Death. "Can you do something so that if there are others with supernatural blood, they won't see you? I don't want to have to explain why you're here."

"Anything for you, *kochanie*." Death nodded and came to the front to exit with her so they wouldn't have to explain why the rear door opened by itself.

By the time Jael and Death came around the ambulance Nathan had already pulled out their medical bag. She snatched the cardiac monitor off the shelf and shouldered it before reaching back in to pull out the stretcher.

"There's no need for any of that." Cleg called to them as he strolled to them. "DOA, the M.E. is on the way."

"Another victim? It can't be Annabell, or we wouldn't have been called."

"Another victim? Annabell? Jael, what the hell is going on?" Nathan looked from her to Cleg.

Her big mouth got not only herself but Cleg in deep this time. She had too many secrets now not to watch what she said around others. Nathan might know her secret but it wasn't her place to tell Cleg's or even about the murders.

Cleg gave a brief nod. "He'll find out eventually. With five murders, the media will be running the story soon."

"Five?" Nathan's eyes bulged with shock. "How do you know about this if no one else does?"

"It's a long story, Jael can explain. First…Jael, I need a minute *alone*." Cleg turned on his heels, stomping away without waiting to see if she followed. Twenty yards off, just far enough out of Nathan's hearing, Cleg stopped and waited for her to join him. "What's he doing here?" He nodded to Death.

She laughed at the worry that lined her twin's face. If he wasn't careful he'd be a wrinkle mess before he was thirty. "He's been following me around like my shadow on a sunny day. Don't worry, no one besides you and Nathan can see him."

"Nathan?" His eyebrow rose up in question.

"Nathan is fae, a healer. Supernatural blood in Nathan allows him to see Death." Now she was telling Cleg what Nathan was when she just told herself she couldn't reveal her brother's destiny, not even to her partner. This was a double standard at its best.

"You've got to be kidding me. I'd have never guessed." Cleg looked to Nathan. "Just keep in mind that anyone with enough supernatural blood can see Death unless he cloaks himself from it. If he's going to follow you around like a damn guard dog, make sure he stays hidden. We could both lose our jobs and worse if anyone finds out what we are."

"I'll make sure he does. Now tell me what you stopped me from seeing." Jael looked off in the direction of the scene. With all the emergency lights highlighting the darkness she couldn't see anything beyond a few vehicles. She had a feeling that it would be like the others from the crime scene photos Cleg showed her. A woman lying on the roof of the car, pieces of her skin torn from her body, her throat slit. If he held to pattern, it would be another blonde in her twenties.

"Amber Brown, twenty-two, from Denver. She was passing through when her car broke down. Just like the others. Has she not appeared to you yet?"

"No. She might still be by her body, watching. Death explained sometimes they do that when they're not ready to leave. Can you get me closer?"

Cleg tipped his head back in a gesture to Death. "You haven't had enough time to gather control over your powers, or you could make yourself invisible to travel through the others unnoticed. However, in the meantime, Death can make you invisible with his touch."

"As long as you maintain contact with me, you won't be seen by others," Death explained.

"Don't do it here." Cleg held up his hand to stop her. "You need to be hidden before you take his hand. Get in the back of the ambulance. Nathan will keep the door open so you can come out without being seen. Whatever you find, do it quick. You won't have much time before someone might wonder where you are."

She gave Cleg a brief nod and headed back to the ambulance. Did Cleg just say that once she had a handle on her abilities, she'd be able to make herself invisible? With a mental note to ask Death about it later, she climbed into the ambulance.

"Will this hurt?"

"No pain, only a weird sensation. Whatever happens, don't let go of my hand. As long as we are touching no one will see or hear you. Remember to avoid other people. Just because we're invisible doesn't mean we wouldn't be felt in some way to them." Death held out his hand to her.

With a quick glance to Nathan to be sure the coast was clear, she slid her hand into his. The coolness of Death mixed with the warmth of her nerves, but nothing else happened.

"It didn't work."

Chapter Five

"It worked as it was supposed to." Death nodded to silver compartments where their reflections should have been. Instead, there was nothing, just the wall behind them.

She held her other hand before her. "But I can still see myself and I don't feel any different."

"You're still on the same plane, just hidden from view, it's why you must be careful when coming into contact with others. As for feeling different, what did you expect?"

"I'm not sure, something. I guess pain or at least a sensation to represent the change." Jael shook her head, uncertain she even understood what she meant. She blamed his touch that sent her thoughts jumbling around her mind and her heart fluttering. She shook it off and got back to the murdered girl waiting for them. "We need to go."

Death nodded, leading the way. "Stay close."

Outside the world seemed a little more gray than normal. The blue streaks that highlighted the world were darker, more real. Was she touching Thanatos more than before? Was she invisible because she was touching the land of the dead? More questions she didn't have answers for, and more she didn't have time to ask.

Weaving between emergency vehicles and personnel, they neared the scene. While some of the police stood around, others processed the crime scene. There in the middle of things was a car with a body laid out against it. The spirit stood not five feet away, tears streaming down her face, watching everyone as they moved.

"There she is," she whispered to Death.

"Let's get closer and get her away from here." Death tugged her hand when she paused, her gaze on the body stretched out on the car. "The body's not going to help, only she can give you the pieces of this puzzle."

A deep breath in and out before she gathered the nerve to continue forward. She didn't know what had been done to the latest victim and honestly she wasn't sure she wanted to know, let alone see it.

"Amber, I'm here to help. Can we talk?"

"You can see me?" The woman stared at them with glossy eyes. When Jael nodded, the spirit continued. "What are you? Why can't anyone else see me? Why did this happen to me?"

"I'm here to help tell your story. We will catch the person that did this to you. Right now I need you to come with me so we can talk." Jael focused on Amber, but she could see from the corner of her gaze that Death surveyed the movements of those around them. Occasionally moving them to the side to avoid contact with someone.

"How are you going to help me?" Amber was clearly suspicious.

"My brother is a detective, he's working this case. I'll tell him what you remember and we'll get the bastard. He's waiting for us."

"We've spent enough time like this, we must go now." Death's words held a touch of urgency to them.

"I can't leave my…" Amber glanced toward her body, now covered with a sheet.

"There is nothing you can do here and you don't need to see them cart your body away. Come with me so we can see justice served."

Amber nodded and stepped forward. That's when Jael noticed her right arm was severed at the shoulder. Severed was putting it mildly, the wound appeared hacked and jagged, making Jael sick to think of the pain the woman went through.

Death leaned in close to her ear, whispering so the woman's spirit wouldn't hear him. "You're seeing her as she died because she's not strong enough to portray a memory of how she was before. The final moments were too horrifying for her not to remember herself that way."

Well, that explained one thing at least. It didn't help her churning stomach, though. She turned, making her way through the crowd, taking Death with her and Amber tailing behind them. The white medical examiner's van pulled up just as they left the throng of vehicles.

"I'm truly dead." Amber's soft voice echoed above all else.

"I'm sorry," Jael whispered before stepping back into the ambulance. Out of sight, she let go of Death's hand, becoming solid once again as she sank down to the bumper.

"That was close timing, Jael." Cleg had his arm crossed over his chest. "I've got to deal with the M.E. If you get another call before I get back, I'll call you when I have a moment."

She nodded. "I'll gather what I can."

"Who was that hunk?" With a moan, Amber undressed Cleg with her gaze.

Jael snapped her fingers in front of the spirit's face, while Death stood next to her snickering. "My twin brother, Cleg. He's the detective I mentioned working this case. Now focus, tell me everything you remember."

Jael leaned her head against the back of the seat, exhausted. Two more calls after the murder scene before their shift was over, and she couldn't wait to crawl into bed and sleep the day away. Just as they pulled into the ambulance bay, she caught a glimpse of Cleg coming out of the police station across the street.

"You deal with him and I'll clock us out." Nathan nodded toward Cleg before jumping out. "Unless he's done I can give you a ride back to your condo."

"Thanks." She didn't want to deal with Cleg, not while completely exhausted, but the images of Amber still burned into her mind. "Cleg," she called, hopping out.

"Just the person I wanted to catch before heading to the M.E.'s office." He jogged across the street, looking just as rundown as she was. "Did you get anything for me?"

"Amber told me the same thing you already know, but the difference is she's from here. I'm sure you already know that. He also hacked her arm to pieces." She shuddered unable to stop the images from coming back to her. "While doing it, he kept going on about how he needed more pieces, his masterpiece wasn't finished. That he was going to immortalize Amber for all eternity. He was turned on by what he was doing."

"None of the others mentioned he was aroused by his actions." Cleg made a note of it in his little black notepad.

"None of them. Amber said he didn't seem aroused until he started cutting her." Jael looked around, making sure no one was close enough to overhear. "She believes he would have raped her if she wouldn't have died first. He didn't cut her throat until she was already deceased and then I think it was only to keep the pattern. She was watching him after the life slipped from her body. There was no longer any amusement for him."

It wasn't her place to judge, but after gathering what she heard from the women she jumped to a conclusion. "Cleg, I believe his kills will continue to escalate. He might rape the next one as he's hacking her to bits. We must find him and quickly." The next woman caught on the side of the road wouldn't be as lucky as Maddie, Amber, and the others.

"The M.E. was able to confirm that vecuronium was used in all women, except Amber, whose blood work isn't back yet. I do agree he's getting more vicious with each kill." Cleg leaned against the ambulance. "Captain has agreed for you to work with a sketch artist. Have Nathan give you a ride home, get some rest, and I'll call you this afternoon about setting up a time for it."

"Okay." She nodded as Nathan came back out onto the ambulance bay. "Cleg, you need to get some rest as well. You won't be any good to the investigation or these women if you're exhausted."

"With the latest body, Captain has assigned Jaz to work with me on this case. I'm going to bring him up to speed after meeting the M.E. and then get a few hours of sleep."

Jaz was Gemma's fiancée, and they lived in the only other condo on the top floor of building. Such an unlikely couple, Jaz was a detective who sometimes worked with Cleg, and Gemma the ADA—assistant district attorney.

Gemma was the first person Jael rented to once she bought the building. A six story old warehouse that sat on the edge of town overlooking the river and city, had been turned into condos a few years ago. They became fast friends and the four of them—Cleg, Jaz, Gemma, and Jael—had started dining together a few times a week, depending on their schedules. Over the last year she had really been able to get to know Jaz, and she trusted him to keep Cleg safe.

Cleg caught her arm. "One more thing, I think you should start carrying again."

Carrying. A year ago, when there was a spike in crime, Cleg had insisted she get her license to carry a concealed handgun. She had carried it when their mother was in the hospital since the parking lot was dark and isolated at night. A chill went through her. "You think it's really necessary?"

"Yes." Cleg nodded and for the first time looked to Death for backup.

"He's right. With the killer aiming at women, and you haven't had time to fully develop and learn your abilities, it might be for the best. I'll be with you until the killer is caught, but even so, having a gun on you would make you safer," Death chimed in. Until that moment she almost forgot he was there. Through most of the night he hung back, letting her do her job.

"I think it's uncalled for, but if my Lieutenant approves it I will. Otherwise it's going to be pointless since I have no plans to leave home at night except for work." She yawned, ready for this to be over so she could get some sleep.

"I'll pull some strings." Cleg tipped his head to signal Nathan. "Be safe, sister, I'll see you in a few hours."

As Cleg strolled back to his police issued SUV, Nathan made his way to her. The sun was teasing along the horizon, threatening them with the light of day. Most people were still tucked into their beds or preparing for work. While Jael would be going to sleep, trying her best to catch up on all she'd lost thanks to Death.

The drive to her condo building took no longer than five minutes but it was almost more than Jael could handle. Her eyelids threatened to close as the tentacles of sleep pulled at her.

"Thanks, Nathan." She was squeezed in between Death and Nathan, uncomfortable in such tight quarters with them.

Death stepped out of the truck, and she started to follow when Nathan placed his hand on her knee. The simple gesture seemed intimate, and sent her heart skipping a beat.

"You sure you don't want me to walk you up?" Nathan asked, his hand on the gearshift ready to put it into Park.

"I'm fine. Thanks. I have my guard dog." She tipped her head back to Death who stood holding the door.

He raised his hand to her face, cupping her cheek and forcing her to look at him. "This is against every rule in the book." Her heart leaped, as he leaned toward her. His breath feathered a caress across her mouth and then he kissed her. Adrenaline flooded through her veins, as she opened her lips allowing him entry to her mouth. His tongue slipped between her lips, the kiss devouring her. It ended as quickly as it began.

Months ago she longed for him to show true interest in her, not the casual flirting that had become second nature between them since he transferred from the fire department. Now things were too unsteady, full of doubt as to what the future would hold.

"Call me later and let me know how things go with the artist." She gave Nathan a quick nod as she used the last remaining energy she had to climb down from the truck. Death slid his arm around her waist and pushed the truck door shut.

Nathan cracked the window and called out, "Jael, make him tell you the prophecy of the Grim Reaper and Death." Nathan pulled away from the curb and drove off.

Puzzled, she looked at Death.

"What is happening between you and the fae?" Death asked.

"My personal life is not your business." She crossed her arms over her chest. If she hadn't been so bone-weary she'd have pushed away from him, and left him standing there alone.

"It is my business. You're the Grim Reaper."

"Don't you have something else to do besides put your nose in my business?"

"My darling, you know he isn't who you want. You're just settling."

She let out a deep exhale and glared at him. "You've been agitated since we left the murder scene, what's going on? What did Nathan mean?"

He tipped his head back, almost as if trying to smell something. "Inside. It's not something to discuss here…" Death's words were cut off by a sudden flash of fire, smoke filling the air with a sickening sulfur smell. Without a thought for her own safety Jael took a step forward, going in search of what caused the flash. Death's grip wrapped around her bicep, stopping her mid-step. "Don't."

"Someone could be injured."

"It's not that type of activity. Just wait." He kept a firm grip on her arm, his gaze searching the darkness next to the building.

"I see your guard dog is firmly in place, daughter." A thick ringing voice cut through the night air seconds before a gentleman appeared. With his black hair combed away from a tight narrow face smooth of wrinkles, he appeared no older than thirty. There had to be some supernatural blood running through the man's veins to allow him to see Death.

Death's body went tense, his fingers digging a little deeper into her skin. "I'm sorry, can I help you?"

He cocked his head to the side in question. "Daughter, you must feel the connection between us."

"I have no idea who you are, but if you don't leave my property I'll call the police." Slipping her hand into her pocket she pulled out her cell phone, ready to make good on the threat. A cool breeze washed over her, blowing her hair away from her face, and at the same time Death stepped in front of her.

"Leave." Death's deep voice crackled with power.

"She is my daughter." The man stepped a little to the side of Death, looking at Jael. "I wish to speak with you, daughter."

His red eyes glared at her through the darkness, capturing her until she felt like she was falling into them. Everything around her seemed to fall away until all she could see was his eyes. Flames danced within, calling to her, offering their warmth against the cool night air.

"Don't look into his gaze." Death was shaking her, trying to pull her back from where she had gone but the warmth was almost too much for her to leave. She felt her skin heat, her mouth go parch with the desire for water, as if she was being burned from the inside out.

Death dug his fingers into her until it hurt and still she couldn't tear her gaze away from him. It wasn't until Death stepped in front of her that she was able to blink, his sapphire eyes blocking her view, the sparkles of silver dancing before her. The coolness of death settled her until she could breathe again. Still he clung to her, his embrace keeping her on her feet.

"I need to sit down." Her voice was barely a whisper but Death nodded.

"You are my daughter and when I tell you I must speak with you, you will make time." The power and anger tainted those words, causing Jael to look at him again. Careful to avoid direct eye contact, she took him in. For a man that was supposed to be the Prince of Darkness he looked unbelievably normal, except for the flames dancing in his red eyes.

"You have no right to demand anything from me. Furthermore I have nothing to say to you." Jael turned to go inside when Lucifer's powers sizzled to life again, casting a wave of heat through the air again.

"Daughter, that was not a suggestion, it was an order. You will speak with me now."

She spun to him, anger coursing through her. "Don't threaten me." A ball of electricity sprang to life, hovering just above her outstretched palm. Staring down at it, she couldn't believe what was happening. "Death…"

"Another ability, it won't harm you, only the ones you direct it at." Death whispered, leaning close so he wasn't overheard, before turning back to Lucifer. "The abilities of the parents were divided between the twins. Jael is not yours, you will not come near her again unless invited."

"Is that what you want?" Lucifer looked to Jael who still held the ball.

Nodding, she moved her hand, letting the electricity bounce, trying to get the feel of this new power. "You might have your claws into Cleg, but you won't do the same to me. I want nothing to do with you or your domain of Hell."

"Child, to go down that path will create enemies you don't want. To keep company with him, you'll only be surrounded by death." Lucifer slid his hand from his jacket pocket.

A low rumble started deep within her, slowly seeping out until it was loud, echoing in the night's stillness. "Surrounded by death, are you kidding me? I'm the freaking Grim Reaper. Death is my life. Now I suggest you leave because as powerful as you are, I promise you I can be one hell of an enemy."

"I wouldn't doubt that for a moment, daughter, but know I always get what I want in the end. It's best not to fight me." He disappeared in a flash of flames and smoke.

"Could my life get crazier? The Devil as a father is just more than I can comprehend tonight." Knowing instinctively what to do she closed her hand around the ball of electricity, putting it out without any pain. "I need to sleep."

"First I believe there's something we need to address about Lucifer." Death slid his arm around her waist and guided her back to the building.

Chapter Six

Once again night had fallen over Crystal Falls when Jael finally woke, her protector Death reclining on a chair next to her bed dozing. She thought back on all the changes in the last few days. She'd gone from an average single woman with a job she loved, to being a Grim Reaper aiding in the search for a murderer. Spirits lingering around her waiting for the killer to be caught and the threat of the killer escalating his tactics to brutal level had her uneasy. If the pattern continued, the murderer would be out searching for his next victim. She pushed off the covers, unable to lay there while a woman was being hunted like prey.

Death's eyelids popped open. Fully awake, he stretched out his legs. "Cleg called, there's an appointment for you the day after tomorrow at eleven with the sketch artist. They had to bring one in from another police department, and that's the soonest they can get one."

"I can't just sit here doing nothing." She swung her legs over the side of the bed, careful to avoid him.

"What are you planning to do? You can't go driving around Johnsonville Road trying to find this lunatic."

Running off halfcocked searching Johnsonville Road hadn't actually occurred to her, and if she was honest she had no idea what she could do to help. But sitting still wasn't an option either. There was no way she wanted to stand over another dead body, or have another spirit arrive with the same story as the others. She had a duty to stop him, to bring justice to the spirits who depended on her.

"I'll call Cleg, see if there's anything I can do."

"He's sleeping. Working round the clock has taken its toll on him. Give him a few hours. Crystal Falls Police have extra manpower on Johnsonville Road. Every able body is searching for the killer. There is nothing you can do but put yourself in danger, and I won't have that."

"Fine, then let's discuss what Nathan meant when he said you needed to tell me the whole story." With the Devil showing up on the stoop of her building, she'd forgotten about it until now.

He leaned back against the chair, watching her intently. "Prophecy says there will be a Grim Reaper that is my other half. We were divided by our enemies when I was brought into this world. When the two halves come together, they'll make a team like no other. They'll join together to conquer the ever growing afterlife population, and she'll become his right-hand to defeat *him*."

She wondered if the bottom would ever stop falling out of her world. It seemed like there was one surprise after another. One wave slamming into her after another until she felt like she would drown. "Him?"

"Who do you think it is?"

"I have no idea, Death. If I knew, why would I ask?" The annoyance peaked through her words.

"The Devil."

His short statement filled her with so many emotions she couldn't put her finger on one. Unease, anger, excitement, and more rolled in the pit of her stomach with those two little words. Her body shook to her very core, thinking of what it would entail to bring down the Devil himself.

"You've got to be kidding?"

"No. Hell is a place for the worst of the worst—the true demons. But he also sinks his claws into many that don't deserve his wrath. He leads them astray days before their death, giving them no time to repent, to make right their sins. He's building an army and the only chance of defeating him is when I find my true Grim Reaper."

She swallowed the lump forming in her throat, but it was near impossible. Her heart pounded frantically in her chest. Her palms were damp with sweat. "Am I the one?"

"*Kochanie*, only you can make that decision." He placed his hand on her knee. "There's a strong connection between us, one I've never experienced with a charge before, but in the end it's you who has to decide. It can't be forced upon you, nor taken back once you've committed. All I ask is you give us a chance. Come to my world and let us explore what could be between us. You'll find the answers to everything you need to know to truly understand what is happening beyond the spirits you help."

His touch boiled the blood running through her veins. In spite of trying to remain calm, her nerves got the best of her as a burst of laughter escaped her lips. "I see ghosts, for Pete's sake, and that's far from being a good fit for any meaningful relationship. No wonder Mom never really dated after..." The words caught in her throat. If she was the Grim Reaper of the prophecy, then she was expected to defeat her father.

"There's no fault with seeing the dead."

"If the Devil is defeated, what does that mean for Cleg?"

"Cleg has to forge his own path. He has options open to him, but you cannot interfere with them. It must be his decision. There are two likely options for him. He can take his place with your father at any time, obeying the laws already in place, or he can join us to defeat Lucifer. If Lucifer is defeated, Hell can be run as Cleg sees fit, or he can forgo his destiny to run the underworld. His decisions will have to be made in time, and like you once his choices are made, it cannot be undone." His fingers teased along the top of her hand, rolling over the mountains of her knuckles. "Your father believes he can sway you over to the dark side as well, giving him both twins and therefore having more control over the earth, spirits, and Heaven. He won't give up, he'll send his demons after you if he must. We need to work on your abilities so when that happens you're ready."

"This is all so much. How will I know if I'm the one?"

"Come to my world and see all I tell you for yourself. It will give you a chance to understand everything before choosing your path."

Going away with him was slightly tempting, but what of the issues she had at hand. To see his world would be an eye-opening experience and a way to learn more, but should she give into the temptation? "You believe I'm the Grim Reaper, your other half, don't you?"

"*Kochanie*, regardless of the connection between us, or my beliefs, it is your decision. I am not to force myself and my world onto you."

"I'll go, but not until whoever is hunting women is caught." While her actions might be insane, Jael had to know what her future held. Was she the Grim Reaper destined to be with Death, or was there another reaper yet to be born to be Death's fate? A twinge of jealousy sank through her at the thought of another with Death.

"Very well, then since you're awake let's work on your abilities. Once you figure out what calls them you should be fine."

"What abilities do I have?"

"The electricity ball you've already discovered. That isn't so much a power of the Grim Reaper, more of one from your heritage, and in time there could be more that develop from your father's blood in you. Ones from your mother are more in tune with the grave. You can travel to Thanatos, or straddle it to make yourself invisible as we did last night. You can stop time, wink out of the place you are and appear in another place. The Grim Reaper has the power to take lives and give life to anyone it chooses. However, when a life is resurrected, a life must end." Death listed off the powers making Jael feel slightly overwhelmed.

How would she handle all of them, not to mention others that might appear because of her tainted blood? What confused Jael was how her mother could mix with the Devil, the one man she had to have known the Grim Reaper and Death would eventually eliminate. Or was that her reason? Did the Grim Reaper who was destined to complete the tasks need the abilities of the Devil himself to do so?

"My mother knew the prophecy of you and your other half, correct?"

"Yes. Why?"

"I'm trying to understand why she would sleep with him." Jael pulled her legs up under her.

"She fell in love with him before she knew what he was. He's the deceiver. You should not blame Ann for it." He laid his hand over hers. "Let's see if we can get your abilities under control. The electricity ball, when you brought that to hand what were you feeling?"

"Anger. He's trying to divide Cleg and I when we've always been a team, that makes me angry. He tried to scare me with his threats, it only made me angrier that he would resort to that. Threaten me or mine and I'll fight like a bear woken from hibernation. It's not a way to get me to do what he wanted." The rage returned with such force the ball of electricity appeared in her palm, bigger and brighter than before.

"Excellent. Your rage is manifested in the ball of electricity." He stood from the chair, pulling her off the bed in one smooth motion. "Come, *kochanie*, let's work on your capability to touch Thanatos."

Standing, she reached out with her other hand, laying it over his heart. The pattern of heartbeats under her fingers intensified from her touch. "Calling me that leads me to believe you suspect I'm your other half, or why else call me your darling?"

"It could be a term of endearment I use with all Grim Reapers."

"It's not." She wasn't sure how she knew but it was almost as though she could taste the lie on her tongue. "You know I'm the one, don't you?"

"It doesn't matter what I believe. In the end it's you that must make the decision."

After hours of extensive training on how to control her powers, Jael was exhausted. Muscles she didn't even know she had hurt. She sat by the coffee machine, impatiently waiting for it to finish brewing, when she heard a key turn in the lock of the front door. Knowing it was either Cleg or Gemma, she didn't move from her perch.

Gemma's heels clattered against the hard wood floors as she made her way up the small hallway that led to the open condo. "Jael, get your lazy bones out of bed…"

"In here." She yawned.

"This place is so dark, how can you see anything?" Gemma flicked the light switch on, shining light into the kitchen.

"Hey, I was enjoying the view. It's not often I'm home to take advantage of the view, all the lights of Crystal Falls twinkling below." She squinted from the blinding light. When she was able to focus again without seeing white spots, her eyes went wide, finding her best friend standing next to the kitchen bar looking like a bad girl gone wild, with a touch of classy hooker thrown in. "What the hell?"

"All five lights our little town has." Gemma raised a perfectly arched eyebrow at her.

Gemma was being slightly dramatic but not by much. Crystal Falls didn't even have a stop light. The cozy town was her home and she loved the view so much she'd purchased the building. There were lights that lined the river and park area, not to mention the ones on each side of Main Street.

"Was there something you wanted, Miss Hooker?"

"It's for the Halloween Ball next month. I wanted to try it out while Jaz was working so he didn't get a sneak peek. You don't like it?" Gemma frowned.

"It's not that…" Jael tried to wrap her mind around the outfit. Her friend was the girl next door, with long, brown hair and a sleek body, but here she stood in a red and black mini skirt with a slit clear up her thigh. Black fishnet stockings, red boots with black lacings to her knees, and a sheer blouse half-buttoned finished the outfit. Her hair was curled and fluffed, and the black eyeliner drew attention to her eyes before the bright red lipstick caught Jael's attention. *Wow!*

"It's so different than anything I expected. You look great." *Girl, you have nerves of steel to go anywhere dressed like that.*

"Jaz is going as a cop and well, I thought I'd dress this way so he can arrest me." She wiggled her eyebrows.

"You better be careful or you'll end up in steel handcuffs and they won't be Jaz's. Does he know you're going as a hooker?" The coffee was finally done. She opened the cupboard door for two mugs.

"No. It's a surprise. I can't wait to see his face. You don't think it's over the top do you?"

Breathing in the sweet, vanilla scent filling the kitchen, she stared at Gemma. "You're definitely over the top." Jael pointed at Gemma's perky bosom peeking out of the top of the blouse. "No, you look great. Halloween is a time to step out of one's comfort zone and be daring."

The Halloween Ball the fire department staged was the second biggest celebration the city of Crystal Falls held each year, only to be beaten by the Christmas Festival. The whole town rallied together for the celebration, and best of all, everyone got into the spirit by dressing up. The ball wasn't just for the children of Crystal Falls, it was actually more for the adults. Though many children attended the ball, their party was on a different night—one that was more kid friendly, after the town's trick-or-treat night. Next month marked the tenth annual ball and Halloween itself. Until Jael was thrown head first into the world of Death and serial killers, she had looked forward to the event.

Thoughts of the ball disappointed her, so she tried to push it aside. She wasn't going to mention to Gemma that she wasn't sure she'd be able to go. If there wasn't some spirit looming around waiting for her help, there was the whole situation with Nathan. Was it fair to go to the Halloween Ball with him when she might be destined to be Death's other half? It felt too much like leading him on, even if he hadn't shown much interest in her in the first place.

Gemma climbed onto the bar stool and crossed her legs, sending the slit in the skirt higher than Jael thought possible. Gemma's leg swung to an unheard beat as she destroyed the precious coffee with loads of hazelnut creamer. "What are you going as?"

Jael leaned against the counter, chuckling. "I'm going as the Grim Reaper. It was Nathan's idea."

Coffee sprayed from between Gemma's lips. "Stepping out of the closest?" She teased. "Ever since you found out and broke the news to me, I thought you would want to keep the fact that you're the Grim Reaper under wraps."

"I do. Who's going to know? Everyone will think I'm just dressed for Halloween. It's perfect."

"Perfect until a ghost shows up."

Her friend's words hit the nail on the head.

"Since Mom passed away, Death and spirits occupy all my free time, but I hope this ball will give me a break. Maybe I can work something out with Death and he can keep the spirits away for a precious few hours. Even the Grim Reaper needs a day off, right?"

"If anyone deserves a ghost break, it's definitely you. What about Nathan, what's he going as?"

"Nathan will be a dead hospital patient that I'm here to collect."

"Morbid, especially for you, but I love it." She wiped her mouth with a napkin and sipped her diluted coffee. "How are you dealing with the whole situation? Is Death still bothering you?"

"I still can't believe I'm the Grim Reaper, but dealing with Death daily sure brings reality home. Every time I see him, it sinks in even more." She was careful not to say Death's name too loud. Whenever she said his name aloud, he'd appear, and she didn't need him here now. This was her first break from him since her powers manifested. All she wanted to do was enjoy a nice cup of coffee and a moment of peace.

"You told me Death was irresistibly good looking, so it can't be that bad."

Irresistible was the understatement of the century. Death was a god, with cheekbones that were chiseled from stone and piercing sapphire eyes sparkling with hints of silver that would draw anyone woman's attention if she could see him. He had an unnatural fascination with black clothing, but then again maybe it added to the portrayal of death. At least he didn't wear one of those long black cloaks.

As if conjured from thought, Death appeared behind Gemma. His six-foot-five build seemed imposing next to her. "We need to talk *now*."

Damn it, what does he want? Jael raised her eyebrow, hoping Gemma wouldn't sense his presence. Ever since she had described Death's haunting magnetism to Gemma, her friend despised the fact she couldn't see him.

Thankfully before Jael had to make an excuse to get rid of Gemma, she rose from the chair and placed her coffee mug in the sink. "I need to change and get some shopping done. I'm glad you're going to the ball with Nathan. We'll have a blast."

Chapter Seven

Jael leaned against the counter, coffee mug in hand, waiting for Death to explain the urgency. His brows were knitted together almost as if he was worried about something.

"What's happening?"

"I'm not sure the killer is human. I believe it might be one of your father's demons on the loose." He moved across the kitchen in a blur, swinging the refrigerator open and grabbing a beer she kept on hand for visitors.

"What? Wouldn't a demon just kill, not skin them? The women described him, and there's nothing demonic about his looks."

"A Pishacha is a flesh eating demon. They have the power to assume different forms at will, or even become invisible. It is possible the Pishacha has possessed a human to do these crimes." Death tossed the beer can in the trash and took a long swig. "Whichever it is, he's taking the flesh to eat. It's highly unusual, normally they'd just eat it on the victim."

"I've got to let Cleg know." She sat her coffee on the counter, and strolled toward the door.

Death caught her arm as she moved past him. "Use your power."

"I don't know…" Worries of appearing inside an object freaked her out. It wasn't hard to step out of it because she was still invisible when she reappeared, until she was sure the coast was clear, but it still felt uncomfortable.

"Take my hand, I'll make sure you don't end up in the bedside table or anything," he teased, holding out his hand to her.

She slipped her hand into his, knowing he'd keep her safe. Instead of holding her hand, he pulled her close, pressing her along the length of her body. His arms around her waist, he stared into her eyes.

"*Kochanie,*" he whispered, seconds before they blinked out of her condo.

The world around her disappeared, replaced by cool air, until they appeared in Cleg's condo one story down. The contemporary furnishings were replaced with more traditional surroundings that had a touch of modern mixed in. Other than the furnishings, the condos were entirely the same, expect Cleg's didn't have a loft. The two bedrooms were just off the living area.

"Not hard if you just focus." The coolness disappeared as they stepped away from Thanatos.

"What the hell?" Cleg stood before them, his service weapon pointed at them.

"Cleg, it's me." She turned in Death's embrace to face her brother, holding up her hands as she said a silent prayer he could see her in the dark condo. A bullet wound because she snuck up on him wasn't in her plans for the night.

"Damn it, Jael! You scared the shit out of me." Cleg lowered his weapon. "What the hell are you doing here anyway, and since when can't you use the door?"

"That would be my doing. I'm trying to get her used to her abilities." Death's arm was still around her waist, holding her to him.

"Fine, then tell me what you're doing here."

"Get dressed and then we can talk." She nodded to the towel tied around Cleg's waist.

He looked down at himself as if he'd just realized he was almost naked, water still dipping from his body. "Give me five minutes. I just got out of the shower when I heard you." He turned on his heels and stalked back to his room.

She wanted to relax against Death's body, to feel the comfort and safety in his embrace. Was her own body confirming her destiny? She wasn't sure and wouldn't give into temptation in the middle of a hunt for a serial killer. Once things were over, the killer was captured and the spirits got the justice they deserved, she would consider her feelings for Death.

"Do you think Lucifer knows there might be a Pishacha killing people in this town?"

"There's very little Lucifer is unaware if. I suspect it might be a challenge to see how Cleg, even you, will handle it. Cleg is the heir to the underworld throne, he'll rule over demons, if he can't control them now then he'll never be able to control Hell." Death's fingers played along the small of her back in an intimate way, slightly unnerving considering what they were discussing.

"Lucifer?" Cleg asked from the doorway of master bedroom, buttoning his shirt.

"Death believes you're looking for a Pishacha for the murders. I asked him if he thought Lucifer knew there might be a demon killing women here."

"Trust me, if that is the case not only does Lucifer know, he most likely is allowing it or at least looking the other way. Do you have any evidence that it's a Pishacha?" Cleg stalked toward them. The dark circles around his eyes had lessened, making him look healthier than he had the last time she'd seen him.

"There was something about the scene that pickled my scenes. While Jael was showering, I went back to Johnsonville Road to see if there was any trace of something I could pick up on. That's when I recognized the scent, from many years ago when I came across one." Death's fingers stilled just above the waistband of her jeans. "Pishacha are voracious flesh-eating demons that are caught in a limbo between Heaven and Hell, somewhat like the spirits you help, Jael. A Pishacha were at one time human, unable to redeem themselves for the terrible sins they committed during their lives. They are cursed to limbo, eating flesh to survive pain free."

"How do we kill a Pishacha?" Jael inquired.

"The only way you can kill one is with a blessed sword, either decapitation or thrusting the sword through the heart. Seeing that we don't have a blessed sword we will have to make due with trapping it in a spirit box."

"Spirit box?" She wasn't sure that she liked the sound of what that implied.

"Some spirits no matter how hard you try will not find the justice they seek. It can make them, how shall I put it…unruly. That leaves us with no other option but to contain them for our safety as well as others." Death looked at Cleg for a moment before returning his gaze to her. "Other spirits might have evil intentions, they don't completely deserve Hell but Heaven isn't an option either. They are left to roam Thanatos until they've earned their way into one or the other. This can also make for dangerous spirits."

"So you trap them in a box for all eternity?" The very thought turned Jael's stomach.

"Until there's another option, yes, but they are unaware. It's like a permanent sleep for them, they'll dream a life they want. Would you rather we allow them to stay here, turning into a poltergeist to harm someone?"

She glared at Death, disappointed that he could think she'd want such a thing. "No. You said the spirits couldn't harm me."

"Harm you, that's correct. If they become a dangerous spirit or poltergeist, they can harm others. The Grim Reaper has a natural protection against all types of spirits. The only exception is when a demon is backing them, feeding them powers to attack. That normally only occurs when a spirit is trying to earn their way into one of the eternal places."

"Now that you two have all that cleared up, can we get back to the reason you popped into my home in the middle of the night?" Cleg glared at them. While Death gave her a lesson on Reaping, Cleg had added his shoulder holster, gun, and badge without her noticing he'd left the room.

"Yes, the Pishacha. Do you even have a spirit box?" She looked back at Death.

"I have them in Nightscape, we'll get one and be ready for the next attack." Death looked down at her. "Accompany me?"

"Nightscape?" She answered his question with her own.

"Ready?" Cleg interrupted. "That means we have to know *where* and *when* before he can kill the next victim."

"Nightscape is my homeland," Death told Jael. "Like Thanatos it's a different plane, and traveling between the two is no different than coming here." Death looked to Cleg before answering his question. "Between the two of you, finding the Pishacha can be done."

"What?" Jael couldn't keep the surprise from her voice or her expression.

"One of your abilities is to see unscheduled deaths—murders. Cleg should be able to track demons that are part of Hell's regime. Any outcasts would be harder, but he might be able to catch a faint trace of them."

"I've got to check in with Jaz, see where the investigation is going. I want you to take Jael to Nightscape, get the spirit box, and get her ready to find the next scene before he kills the woman." Cleg grabbed his jacket off the back of the couch, and slipped it on. "We need to catch him before we have another dead body at our feet."

"Be safe, Cleg," she called to him as he neared the door.

"It's not me he might be after." Cleg opened the door and disappeared to the other side before shutting it behind him.

"What did he mean by that?"

"It's possible the Pishacha was released by your father, possibly to make you scared enough to embrace your connection to him, or worse to kill you if you rejected him. Now shall we go to Nightscape?"

She shook her head. "First tell me how I will know when there's an unscheduled death?"

"You have to focus, you'll feel the life slipping from them, the fear. No matter how far away they are, you can feel it. This will be closer so it will be easier. There's also a physical pain for some Grim Reapers, normally a stabbing in the stomach, others feel what the victim is going through."

She took a step back, out of Death's embrace, her eyes wide. "I might feel everything that happens to them if I do this? To feel their skin sliced from their body? You can't ask that of me, it's too much."

"It's your choice. You know the consequences if you don't." He leaned close to her, bringing his face to just above hers. Before she could ask what he was doing, he kissed her. Pressing his lips to hers, the heat blossomed until it was a raging fire. Their kiss was anything but sweet and timid like a first kiss normally is, instead it was hot and heavy. They kissed with a frenzy, each drinking the other in as if they were dying of thirst. She couldn't get enough of him.

He broke the kiss, leaving her weak in the knees. "See what you can have with me, *kochanie?*"

Oh, crap!

"Now can we go to Nightscape?" he asked, holding out his hand to her.

"Tell me about it." She refused to take his hand. Answers were needed before she could travel to a world that could hold more danger.

"Nightscape isn't a place to be fearful of. No harm will come to you while you're there. Nightscape is a plane that things like myself have made their home."

"Things?"

"Beings brought into this world by a thought. Those of us who still serve a purpose reside in Nightscape. We've made our homes throughout the plane. Growing up, children believe in Santa, Cupid, the tooth fairy, Mother Nature, and everyone else." He slid his hands into the front pockets of his jeans. "We have all divided the plane into our own areas. I promise you'll come to no harm."

"You're telling me they exist?"

"Why not? It's people believing in them that keeps them alive. Once people stop believing, they disappear or possibly change to something new if there's something that is needed. Now is not the time for any of this. We need to get the spirit box before he attacks again. It's getting late so we need to be quick in case he attacks tonight."

"What about you? If people stop believing in you, will you vanish?"

"No. We are a key part in how life and death works. Even if no one believes in me I serve a purpose. I will always be here."

There was another nail in the coffin as to why they couldn't be together. When she was nothing but dust in the ground he'd still be here, training another Grim Reaper. Unlike him she wasn't immortal, eventually she'd die, and there was no way around that.

Chapter Eight

It took a moment for her eyes to adjust to her new surroundings, to see through the gray and blue streaks. The heat hit her, making it hard to breathe. *I'm in hell, Death lied to me. Shit, I made a mistake.* She pulled away from him in fear.

"Damn it, Thunder!" Death hollered, vibrating the walls around them. "Thunder is always playing tricks on people. He knows some of the Reapers in the past have thought they were working for Hell at first, and this is his way of freaking you out."

"Thunder?"

"He's Mother Nature's son." He slid his arm around her waist. "Welcome to my home."

The beautiful white marble floors had silver swirled through it. The walls were a deep shade of wheat, with an accent wall the color of warm brandy. Everything was homely and welcoming. None of it was like she pictured. It was too bright, too airy. She'd imagined lots of black. After all, that was what Death seemed to favor.

The whole place was completely open, a large king size bed dominating the far wall. The bed was more surprising than the rest of the space. It was covered in a sapphire comforter that matched his eyes, blue, white, and silver pillows decorating the bed. Amongst it all the black headboard had silver swirls mixed in, and it caught her attention the most.

"Not what you were expecting?"

"I'm that transparent?" She spun around, taking in everything. "It's beautiful, just so unlike you."

"You called, my Lord?" A man with shoulder length black hair with what looked like bleached strips through it appeared just off the kitchen area. The white in his hair gave him an aged look, but he couldn't have been older than his early thirties.

Death stalked toward the other man. "Thunder, I can't believe you, and don't call me that. We go through this with each new Reaper, leave Jael alone."

"But…my Lord." Thunder bowed, a full one nearly in half.

"Thunder, I'm warning you."

Jael couldn't help but laugh at the situation. Thunder was doing her best to make her believe she could be working for the Devil himself. The laughter abruptly stopped when the men looked at her. "Thunder, I know who you are. Your antics won't make me run from here screaming. I have already met Lucifer and have promised him that if he wants a fight I'll give him one."

"Ahh, a Reaper who can handle herself, I like that." Thunder winked. "I've heard what's happening, so I'm sure you have a lot to attend to. If you need someone to watch your back you know where I am." Thunder popped out, leaving them alone again.

"I'm sorry about him. Thunder loves practical jokes. A new Reaper is the best entertainment for him, it breaks up the monotony of eternity. Make yourself at home." He strolled across the room to the large mahogany bookshelves, one on each side of the fireplace. As he studied the bookshelf, she realized there was something missing.

"Windows."

He slid a book off the shelf and turned to her. "What?"

"There are no windows."

"Correct. There's no view as in your world unless it's constructed. Using magic you could have a view, but I didn't see the point since I'm between the planes so much. The best thing about Nightscape is places can be changed in a blink, views, bedrooms, anything you want can be changed."

It seemed unbelievable to her. After everything she'd seen and heard, she was still having problems comprehending that he could change his home to fit his needs. "I found it odd, but it has nothing to do with me."

"Actually it has everything to do with you. If you join with me, this will be your home too."

Her jaw fell open. Every time she thought the surprises were over, the ground fell out from under her again. "Are you saying I'd have to give up everything I've worked for? My condo building, my job, friends, Cleg…"

"Not give up, just distance. You can travel between the planes anytime you wish, but once the bonding has taken place you would be more of a target than you are. If you choose me, Lucifer will see you as the ultimate threat, he will seek to destroy you before we can abolish him. Staying in Nightscape when possible will keep you safe."

Slightly lightheaded, she made her way to the couch. The heels of her boots clicking against the marble was almost deafening. "No matter what I feel, nothing can happen between us. You're immortal, I am not. There's no escape from death. One day I'll die, just as all the other Grim Reapers have before me. That is not fair to you. Nor is it fair for you to ask me to stand against Lucifer when it surely means my death."

"I must see Abaddon for the spirit box." He came to her, book in hand.

"The destroyer." She wasn't sure how she knew, but Abaddon meant *the destroyer*. Maybe it was because she understood every language, even ancient ones, or maybe she'd heard the name before. At that moment, she didn't care.

"He's not what you might think." He smirked. "His name leads you to believe otherwise, but he's reasonable."

"Isn't he part of Lucifer's regime?"

"Abaddon is like you, he was Lucifer's first child, born of mixed blood. Some folklore is just that, lore, and the information is wrong. He's called the destroyer because he could raise the dead with a wave of the hand and destroy more than mountains. He can destroy everything anyone holds dear and more."

"Are you picturing Abaddon in some dark underground world, with fire and brimstone? If so, *kochanie*, you couldn't be more wrong.

If you want, you could come with me. I just thought you'd prefer to read this while I'm away. It will answer your questions." He held out the book to her. "We'd make a wonderful pair."

She took the book from his hands. There was magic to the book that sang to her, warming under her touch. The smooth leather under her fingers, the rough binding and jagged pages let her know the book was old. Opening it she found the pages faded with time but the handwriting clear as if preserved for the reader. He disappeared without a word as she thought of what would happen if they joined together. If he impregnated her, she would pass the gift to her child.

Having Death's child was more than she was willing to commit to now. What kind of world would that be, stuck forever in Nightscape, no other children to play with? To be removed from all the wonderful things she experienced growing up, surrounded by immortals that her and the child would never live up to. None of it got them past the fact that she would still be dead before she could fulfill the prophecy.

Jael sat curled up on the sofa reading for what seemed like hours when Death finally returned. Completely overloaded with information and questions, she was pleased to see him. Setting the book aside, she looked up to see him holding a wooden box with symbols carved into it.

"You were gone a while, is everything okay?"

He glanced at his watch. "I was only gone fifteen minutes."

"That's not possible. I've read that book twice to make sure I didn't miss anything."

"Sometimes time moves differently in Nightscape than on your plane. My watch is bespelled to stay in sync with your land." He sat the box on the coffee table and sank down next to her. "Did you learn everything you wanted?"

"Is this all true?"

"Yes. It was all written when I was thought into this world. Only after the completion of the book was I made aware of the prophecy. Do you have any questions?"

She stared at him for a moment before a burst of laughter erupted. "More questions than you can believe, but I think I need to wrap my mind around this first." She dragged her hand through her hair, tugging her way through the loose curls. "It's hard to believe I could become immortal, let alone actually stand a solid chance against defeating the Devil. It's so unbelievable."

He slid his arm around her shoulders. "Has it helped you make your decision?"

Her emotions where in torment she had no idea what she wanted any longer. It was all too much, sending her heart and mind in two different directions. For the first time since she met Nathan her heart wanted someone else—Death. Her mind kept screaming it was too illogical and Nathan was safe. Was there such a thing as safe any longer?

"I need more time."

He nodded, a touch of disappointment in his gaze. "You have all the time that you need. Regardless of the connection between us, the steps you take must be your choice. I am not to force myself and my world onto you."

She rested her head against his shoulder, cuddling against his hard body. She was quite aware that her actions were a contradiction to her words, and sending mixed signals wouldn't help, but in that moment all she wanted was his comfort. In time she'd work though her emotions and come to the right decision. For now she wanted to enjoy the moment.

"Let me show you what could be between us." He leaned into her, pressing his lips to hers, not allowing her a chance to deny him. He tasted of cinnamon, making her crave more of him.

Maybe it was because she realized each day was a gift, not a given right. She left her fears behind, threw caution to the wind, and returned his kisses without hesitation. After giving in to her desire, she would never be the same. Life as she knew it, and the woman she'd been before, would be gone. Driving her tongue between his lips, she devoured him.

He pulled back enough to break there kiss, his mouth still hovering over hers. "I take it that's a yes."

She nodded. The passion controlling her didn't allow her to rethink what they were about to do or to change her mind. He didn't give her time, scooping her into his arms. "The bed is a better place to show you."

His lips reclaimed hers as he carried her. Tugging his black T-shirt from his jeans, she slid her hand under it, touching his chest. Gently he laid her on the mattress, their lips separated and she used that moment to pull his shirt over his head. Baring creamy white skin, and his perfectly chiseled chest as if made of stone.

"I want you naked." He grabbed hold of her sweater, slowly pulling it up her body and over her head. "You had your time, now it's my turn to explore." He kissed her neck, nibbling down her jawline to her shoulder. She unbuckled his belt and slid it out of the loops. It landed on the floor with a thump. She let him have a few more minutes of exploration, since he'd finally made it to her breast. His fingers slipped between the thin fabric and her skin, teasing over the nipple and pushing the bra aside.

She reached behind her, unhooking the bra. Her nipples had always been extra sensitive, the slightest touch bringing her pleasure. He lowered his mouth to her nipple, his gaze locked on her. She moaned in ecstasy when his tongue flicked over one hardened tip. She tugged on his jeans before he could move lower.

"These need to go." She unbuttoned them, gliding them gently over his hips.

"Then yours need to go as well, *kochanie*."

While he slipped the jeans the rest of the way off, kicking out of his shoes, she rose up, stripping the remaining clothes off quickly. Her body craved his touch and it had been too long since she felt the gentle caress of a man. He pulled his mouth from hers and kissed a path down her neck. Sensations collided and threatened to overwhelm her when he teased her nipples. Pushing her gently back onto the bed, his bulky frame hovered above her and he stared down at her, desire burning in his eyes.

He caressed every inch of her body, sending moans of ecstasy from her lips. His touch was incredibly tender, as though trying to memorize every curve of her body with his hands and mouth. Heat soared through her blood, like a fire burning just below the skin, impatient and demanding.

He blazed a hot, wet trail of kisses across her belly and stroked her thighs with his fingertips. With every touch, she arched her hips, demanding more. She couldn't get enough of him. It was if her body was making claim to him, even if her mind hadn't made the decision. Nudging her legs farther apart, his fingers delved inside her and she met the teasing thrusts. A demanding moan she barely recognized vibrated in her throat. The trail of wicked kisses tingled over her thighs. He moved his hand and replaced it with his mouth. Tiny nips and gentle licks flicked over her sweet spot, nearly driving her over the edge. She grabbed his hair, torn between pressing him closer and dragging him up. She wanted all of him.

"Death, please I need you." Even in the sexual haze, she realized what she said and those few words changed everything. Sex would complicate things further if she chose not to align herself with him in the battle against Lucifer. It would also make things harder for her to watch him, knowing that he was destined for another.

This action would give her heart to someone she might never be able to completely have. There would be no going back, but in that moment she didn't care, she wanted him inside her.

"Anything for you, *kochanie*." He spread her legs farther, giving him the access he needed before filling her slowly, inch by inch. Halfway in, he slid out before thrusting back in, filling her completely with his manhood. His strokes fed her fire like tinder set to dynamite. Their magic mingled, making the air thick with it, until their skin glowed from it. Magic of death and life, coming together as one, blazing between them until it lit up the room like fireworks in the night sky.

His hips increased pace, driving the force of each pump. The erotic dance amped up her tension, every delicious glide of his shaft inside her seemed to set off another cascade of heat. Their bodies rocked back and forth, tension stretching her tighter as she fought for the release she longed for. Upon that release, she dug her nails into his back, arching her body into his. He pumped twice more and shouted her name as he found his own ecstasy. Eternity stretched on until he collapsed beside her.

Her breath slowly returned to normal and Death cuddled her against him, caressing her with long, lazy strokes.

Pain erupted in Jael like a volcano. Her whole body felt like it was on fire. The insides of her were boiling, scalding her from the inside out. It was like nothing she ever felt before and she couldn't hide it. She screamed in pain, wiggling on the bed as if to put herself out. Only then did she realize the bright light filling the room was from her. She was glowing a reddish, yellow light from deep within her, illuminating her skin and the room.

"What's…happening to me?" She cried out through clenched teeth.

He held her tight against his body as she thrashed about. "Oh, *kochanie*."

She had a brief second to realize his touch didn't relieve the pain as it had when she came into her powers before the agony intensified. The pain was like nothing she felt in her life, pure torture. She wished her body would go into overload and pass out, but it seemed like there was no such luck. Screams tore through her lips until she was hoarse.

"*Kochanie*, I can't take the pain from you, but you can. Focus." He crouched over her, pinning her to the bed. The fact she hadn't felt him move let her know how out of it she was.

Focusing seemed to be impossible, but she tried to get her mind together enough to remember what it was like to be pain free and willed it to be so again. Her eyes burned hot until all she could see was flames before them. She craned her neck to look at Death. Through the flames she could see him, his eyes wide. Before she could ask what was happening the flames shot from her eyes in a wave, expanding to hit everything in her vision.

The flames sent Death flying off her, across the room to slam into the coffee table, cracking his head on it. "Embrace the chill of death." He blew a wave of cool air at her.

Pushing herself into a sitting position she met the breeze, willing it to cool the flames burning within her. As if her body knew she couldn't take any more heat, it accepted the cold, letting it slide through her, putting out all the fires within her. No longer did flames dance in her vision.

The burning inside was replaced with cold, frost coating her veins, her breath emerging in visible puffs. The chill traveled through her body, coating everything within her, until finally reaching her heart.

I'm going to die. Her mind raced with fears of what would happen now. Who would take over as the Grim Reaper, since there was no women left of her line? Would the spirits be cursed to spend their days wandering Thanatos unable to cross over? Sometime during all that had happened, she'd accepted her legacy, her duty to defeat Lucifer, and it wasn't until the thoughts of her final moments that she truly realized it.

She expected more pain at the frost that stole the life from her, but there was none. The only fear she had was not for herself but for those that depended on her, for Cleg and Death. She collapsed onto the bed, not fighting it as the life slipped from her veins. Inside her chest her heart stopped beating, and she let her eyelids close as she waited for the last bit of life to slip away. Would she be one of the spirits stuck in Thanatos, since the killer was still out there? It didn't matter, there was nothing she could do about it now, only hope that Cleg caught the murderer, and then maybe her and the other women would cross over together.

Chapter Nine

Minutes ticked until she felt the mattress shift until Death's weight, and he took her hand in his. "You're not dying. Open your eyes, *kochanie*."

"I'm not?"

"Not as in the end of things, no."

"Then what happened? What was the fire? The chill? More importantly why isn't my heart beating?" She put her hand over her heart, confirming what she already knew. There was no longer a heartbeat. She had died.

"You've come into the rest of your abilities, including those of your father's blood. Hellfire. The chill of death. You're immortal."

It took her a moment to realize he answered all of her questions in one breath, because at first it sounded like he was rambling. "Let's slow down here and start with one thing. What the hell is Hellfire?" She started with the simplest and left the *immortal* comment hanging between them, not ready to face that one just yet.

"Hellfire is an ability of Lucifer. In simple terms you are taking the fires of Hell and using it. It was burning you because of your fear, which is why I gave you the chill of death. Otherwise it would have burned you alive."

"Why did this happen?"

"I believe while we were cuddling you began to accept the prophecy, and it forced the rest of your powers to manifest in order for you to become immortal. It's why there was such an onrush of Hellfire through your veins, not to mention your eyes."

A vision of his flying through the air sparked in her mind, and the fear that she injured him returned. "I didn't mean to…are you okay?"

"I'm fine, *kochanie*. It takes more than a bump on the head to get me down." His thumb teased along her knuckles. "Are you ready to discuss the fact you're immortal?"

"If I said no, would it go away?" She smirked, not ready to face it.

"You've accepted the life that's supposed to be your destiny or you wouldn't have made the change. Why the second thoughts now?"

"You told me I would be immortal, not that my heart would stop beating. What am I supposed to do for the yearly physicals the department requires? I can't hide the missing heartbeat."

"It can be replaced with magic. I'll show you. It seems to be more than a missing heartbeat that's put the terror in your eyes."

She scooted up in bed, resting against the pillows, and tugged the blanket over her again, covering her nakedness. She took a moment to think about it before answering him. "It's the fear of the unknown. It was one thing having spirits depend on me to help them cross over, but now the duty to defeat Lucifer is on my shoulders as well. What will happen to Cleg if I destroy Hell?"

"Cleg's decisions are his own, but he has a number of options. The biggest ones are that the bond between twins will keep him on our side, and when Lucifer is defeated Cleg would rule. Hell will never be destroyed but it could be changed. Hell was only supposed to be the eternal place for those who truly deserve it—murderers, rapists, child abusers, and demons. It was not for those who were led astray right before their deaths, giving them no time to repent. Cleg's other strong possibility would be to follow in Lucifer's steps keeping Hell as it is."

"That will make him my enemy, leaving me no option but to eliminate him as well." Her voice was low as she came to terms with more devastations in her future.

"I wouldn't worry about any of that now. Your mother instilled exceptional values in both of you, I doubt your brother will pick up where Lucifer left things. Now that your new abilities are unleashed you should be able to sense possibilities of things that might happen, as well as certainties in a person's life. Being twins, Cleg's choices should be clearer to you."

"How will I tell?"

"When you see him, open yourself up, let your shields fall, and you'll feel them. If there's more than one option they will follow suit." He let go of her hand and moved to lie next to her, tugging the blanket away.

"What are you doing?"

"We were interrupted before…" His fingers trailed along her side, brushing gently along her hip, and for the first time she realized he no longer felt like a cold chill.

"Your touch, it's warmer." She placed her hand over his, feeling it to again to make sure. Before he had been cool to the touch against her warm skin, but now there was no difference. "How?"

"You're no longer human, your body temperature is the same as mine. Cool because of the grave chill." Death lowered his face until it was inches above hers. "I'm glad you've made this choice, *kochanie.*" Thunder erupted behind them, making Jael jump.

"Your Grim Reaper is finally among us."

Death tugged the blanket over them before rolling off her giving her a clear look at who stood behind them. She recognized Thunder immediately. Even without the white highlights in his otherwise ebony hair, he was unmistakable. The man standing next to Thunder sent a chill down her spine. His black hair cut short against the skull, his eyes were just black holes glaring at her.

"Thunder, I expect this of you, but not you, Abaddon. Why can't you use the door like normal people?" Death reclined next to her as if he didn't have a care, and cuddled her against his body. "Jael, that's Abaddon. Abaddon, quit looking imposing and say hello to Jael."

"It's a pleasure to meet you, Jael." Abaddon nodded to her.

"Umm…you too." She felt extremely uncomfortable naked in bed with Death while Thunder and Abaddon stared at them from the foot of the bed. "I don't intend to be rude, but is there a reason you're here?"

"We've come to meet you now that you're one of us." Abaddon stated it as if it should have been clear.

Death let out a deep laugh, his chest rumbling under her hand. "I highly doubt this is the opportune time, we have a murderer to catch, so if you'll excuse us."

"That really isn't your job, is it?"

Death glared at Abaddon, a heat of anger to it. "You of all people know we cannot leave the Pishacha roaming free to kill more innocents. Jael is helping to deliver the message from the victims, I am only overseeing her safety."

"She doesn't need your protection any longer, she is immortal now."

"Immortal does not mean she cannot be harmed, nor that she can't be destroyed. You know there are ways for someone to destroy the immortal. I will not stand by and do nothing while she's in danger. There seems to be more to this, Abaddon, so out with it. We have other things to do." The tension between Death and Abaddon was thick enough to cut through.

"There are certain steps *she* must take before she is capable of defeating Lucifer. The fact that she has accepted the prophecy this quickly does not change the fact the steps still need to be achieved. You cannot stand in her way."

Death's body tightened under her embrace. "Abaddon, I know the future better than you do. You will not come into my home and insult me."

"I only speak the truth."

Death shot up, the blanket falling away from them as he got out of the bed. Jael looked down to find she was now clothed in a beautiful pale blue silk chemise nightshirt, and Death wore a pair of black pajama bottoms.

Thunder laid his hand on Abaddon's shoulder. "I believe we should go."

The men continued to stare at each other, neither of them backing down, and Jael took it upon herself to end the situation before it got out of hand. "Abaddon, I'd take his advice. Now isn't the time for this. I need to return to my world to help stop this killer. So if you would kindly leave, I'm sure we can arrange for us to meet again once this is over."

"As My Lady wishes." With one final glare at Death, Abaddon nodded and they disappeared, leaving them alone.

"What the hell was that about? Why did he call me *My Lady*? It's too formal no matter how old he is." She slid out of the bed, putting her feet on the floor and noticed the floor felt warmer than she did. Her new body temperature was going to take some getting used to.

"You're right, we should return." He stalked away toward the walk-in closet.

"Answer me, what's going on?" She went to him, laying a hand on his arm.

He spun around to look at her. "As I told you, Abaddon is Lucifer's child, your brother. Even though centuries separate the two of you, Lucifer gave his kingdom to Cleg and by doing that, even though you have your own destiny, you are still the Mistress of Hell. To say there is some resentment to that is an understatement. I had planned to prepare you for that before meeting him, I never expected him to show up here before I had a chance."

Mistress of Hell? Once again the rug was pulled out from under her feet.

He slid his arm around her waist, drawing her close to his body. "Before you ask…about the steps you have to take before going up against Lucifer. Once he knows you're against him, he will send three demons after you. Each one worse than the first. We'll have to defeat them, therefore gaining more control over your abilities, and powers from the demon."

"Is the Pishacha the first then?"

"No. I believe Lucifer is leaving the Pishacha wreak havoc as a test to you and Cleg. To see what each of you will do. Cleg as the heir to Hell's throne should gain control of the demon and return him to hell. If he allows us to contain him in the spirit box, Lucifer will take it as proof that he needs to drive a wedge between the two of you. It will also confirm your stance on the situation."

Great. Now she had to survive three more demons before taking on the Prince of Darkness. That couldn't be harder than going up against the Devil himself, could it?

The sun was peaking over the horizon when Jael and Death appeared back in her condo. Though the night had been mostly enjoyable for her, to say the least, she couldn't help but wonder what happened in her absence.

"I should call Cleg to see if there was another..." The word 'murder' pressed on her tongue until it was heavy and her mouth was dry.

"Open your senses." She looked at him, not understanding what that had to do with calling Cleg. "He's downstairs."

"Very well. Do you want to come with me?"

He sat the spirit box on the table and held his arm out to her. "Let's be on our way, *kochanie.*"

She took his arm with a warm smile. He was truly a gentleman, one she had sought after for a long time. *I was looking in all the wrong places. My handsome gentleman wasn't among the living, but Death himself.*

A second later she was standing just beside the coffee table in Cleg's apartment. Her brother was at the dining room table, going over the files of the case, no doubt looking for the missing piece of the puzzle that would be the key to catching the Pishacha before he killed again. Dark circles had returned to haunt his eyes. Had he gotten any sleep?

"Cleg?" She kept her voice low, trying not to startle him.

He looked up from the papers. "I'm getting the impression you won't be using the door often now that you have discovered your abilities. Why didn't I get a handy ability like yours? Instead, when I want to disappear and appear at will, the sickening smell of sulfur surrounds me, along with the flames of Hell."

"If it were up to me, I'd be a normal woman. No abilities, demons after me, or any of this." The only regret she'd have if she could give it all up would be losing Death. Not that she should linger on it since there was no chance she could give it up, and she wasn't completely sure she would if it meant losing him. She had people to protect that counted on her, and demons to eliminate. "Was there another tonight?"

"No." Cleg dragged his hand across his face. "It's the first night since this started there wasn't a murder. At least we haven't found one yet. I've been sitting here by the phone all night waiting. It hit the eleven o'clock news. Captain's got major manpower out there watching, trying to keep the town safe. Something seems off to me. I don't think the Pishacha stopped because of news coverage, so why no activity tonight?"

Not that she wasn't grateful for the lapse in his routine, but she was wondering the same thing. Something in her gut told her the change meant the next one would be worse. "That's the million dollar question."

"What are you doing here anyway?"

"We just returned from Nightscape and I wanted to see if there were any developments. There's been no new spirits but sometimes that doesn't mean anything. Some cling to their bodies like a lifeline until it's buried." She stepped closer to the table to look at the files.

Before she could get a good look at most of it, Cleg began to gather it up.

"You don't need to see this stuff." The protectiveness was clear in his voice.

"I don't need to be protected, and there might be some insight I have that you haven't seen yet. Let me help." Cleg had always been protective of her, sheltering her when he could. No girl could ask for a better brother than Cleg. They were a team, one for all and all for one.

Lucifer might take him away from me. The thought of Lucifer made her look at Cleg. Taking in everything about him, not just the features they shared or the ones from their mother. She was searching for any clues as to how much of their father he had within him.

He left the stuff on the table, but eyed her with interest. "You've just returned from nightscape? Does that mean…?"

"The spirit box is upstairs. We'll be ready with it," Death replied while Jael read one of the reports.

"I was speaking of the prophecy."

The breath rushed from her lungs, every muscle in her body frozen. He knew. "I…I think we should focus on the case." In the middle of a murder investigation she didn't want to discuss this, especially not if it was going to create problems.

"Jael, always the worrier." Cleg laid his hand over hers. "I've known since I've found out that you would eventually take Mom's place as the Grim Reaper. Just now when you appeared I knew it was you the prophecy spoke of. I can see the change in you, the power in you would have me doubting myself if I was an enemy. I also know that this change of status will put you in more danger than before. It also means you will go up against Lucifer."

Death came up behind her chair and laid his hand on her shoulder. "On my honor, I will protect her."

"I don't doubt that." Cleg shook his head. "Lucifer will not give up, he'll send everything at you in order to preserve his own skin."

"I know, and no matter what happens, you mustn't get involved," Jael said.

"What?" Cleg pushed back from the table, his eyes wide as if she'd dumped cold water over his head.

"Getting involved will only make you a target as well. As the heir to Hell it could make things extremely difficult for you." Jael leaned forward, no longer interested in the files that were scattered across the table. "You need to think of what will happen once Lucifer is abolished, interfering with what he does to me won't help you when things are over."

"You are my twin, the other half of me. There's no chance I won't be by your side. I never asked to be the heir."

Part of her rejoiced at Cleg's statement. To hear nothing would come between them was heavenly. She couldn't be foolish enough to believe that their father would do everything in his power to divide them and he might succeed. What they needed to do was think of the larger picture, the best way to get out of this without too much physical and emotional pain.

Chapter Ten

Two hours later and after more cups of coffee than Jael could count, she finally finished looking over the files, M.E. reports, and crime scene photos. They were no closer to a clue as to where the Pishacha was holed up at or who the next victim would be.

"We should get some rest, tonight he might attack and we need to be ready." Cleg's cell phone rang. "I need to take this, it's the Captain."

Death laid a hand on her shoulder, giving it a gentle squeeze. "He's right. You should sleep, your body has been though a lot. Exhaustion will creep up on you and we need you ready if the Pishacha attacks."

"Later, there's got to be something we're missing." She shuffled back through the files, trying to find the reports for the latest victim.

"We've gone over them, you've questioned the women, there's nothing another look through the reports are going to produce. Being immortal doesn't mean you don't need sleep." He rubbed her shoulders, easing the tension away. "Over the centuries you will begin to need less, but right now you still need the sleep of a human, or at least nearly."

Cleg returned before she could let her exhaustion force her to agree with Death. "After hearing about the last victim, the sketch artist drove in early and is waiting for us at the station. Sleep will have to wait."

"Very well." Jael stood, stretching out her muscles. "At least if there's an image, maybe the other officers can be on the lookout. Release it to the media and the Pishacha will only change forms leaving us back at square one."

"The Captain agreed it will not be released. The artist has been told you saw the man when Maddie was murdered. It will explain why you have information that no one else does. Only the Captain and I know the truth, and I'd like to keep it that way." Cleg grabbed his gun and shoulder holster off the table and slipped it back on.

Jael looked down at herself. The blue jeans and cream sweater were not going to cut it for the Montana cold. "My coat is upstairs."

Death glanced at her, magic coating the air until a warm winter coat of brown suede appeared on her shoulders, falling mid-thigh. It was beautiful. "Thank you."

"You're welcome. Let's do this so you can get some sleep before night falls." Death wrapped his arm around her back, his fingers resting just along her hip bone.

Cleg paused before slipping on his own jacket. "I doubt I could get you to leave her side, but if you're to accompany her, cloak yourself so no one besides us can see you. The Captain is a

Hellhound, he would see you for sure, and you wouldn't be able to stay with her."

Death nodded. "No one will know I'm there but yourself and Jael."

"I've done some research on Hellhounds and I've found nothing of them being able to appear human. Also why is he here instead of in Hell or guarding one of the entrances to the world of the dead, like a graveyard?" Jael inquired before Cleg could open the door. If any of the condo residents were around, she didn't want them overhearing the conversation.

"Captain Henningsen has a taint of human blood running through him. It allows him to shift at will. He's hiding from Lucifer, so if you see our father don't mention it." Cleg turned the doorknob but didn't open it. "Before you ask, he's in hiding because Lucifer wants him dead. His father gained the ability to shift by killing a demon, and he used that to find a woman to satisfy his needs. Lucifer took it as an insult, killing the father, and now there's a blood price on Henningsen's head."

"Last question, I swear." She gave Cleg a quick smile and dove right in before he could stop her. "Being the heir to Hell, he's okay working with you? Isn't he concerned that you'll tell Lucifer where he is?"

"Henningsen saved my ass. I was still green, just on the police force when there was a shootout with a suspect after a bank robbery the county over. I would have died that day—if it's even possible—if it hadn't been for Henningsen. From then on, he took me under his wing, and it's the reason I've made Lead Detective at such a young age. So no there's no chance I'd inform Lucifer, and if he ever found out I'd fight for Henningsen as he did for me." Cleg opened the door and stepped into the hall before she could say anything else.

She remembered that shoot out well. Their mother was a wreck with worry since both Cleg and Jael were on duty, each of them at the scene. Phone calls from Ann went unanswered until things were done. Jael even remembered the very moment where Henningsen pushed Cleg out of the way, just as bullets came flying toward them. Putting the pieces together she figured Henningsen must have some foresight into the future.

Jael let the cold fresh air blow over her and through her hair, letting it take away the stress of the last hour. While the officers went through shift change, she stood there trying to relax.

Sitting with a sketch artist had seemed so simple when she agreed to it, but it was anything but. Coming into more of her abilities had forced her to relive the experiences the women suffered at the hands of the demon as she described him to the artist. Maddie's spirit had been there to provide details Jael might have forgotten or missed, and to confirm the final sketch, even though after they started she realized it was unnecessary thanks to Jael's newest curse. She tried to let the horrors go, but they clung to her like a wet blanket, tearing at her heart and soul. The images would forever be burned into her memory as if she suffered through them herself.

"Jael?"

A familiar voiced distracted her. She opened her eyes to find the perfect Gemma standing beside her. "Hi, Gemma, what are you doing here?"

"Working on a case involving a car thief." She pushed her shoulder briefcase up a little higher. "I wanted to talk to you, do you have a few minutes? We could grab a cup of coffee."

"Sure, but I can't stay long."

Out of the corner of her eye, she saw Death shake his head. He wanted her to get some rest before nightfall and Jael had already had more than enough caffeine.

She led the way down Spring Avenue, the main street in Crystal Falls, to the town's only coffee house, Morning Joy. It was the perfect play on words since coffee was the morning joy and Joy was the owner's name. Morning Joy was a cozy little café where everyone knew one another. The coffee and food was good, but the atmosphere and conversation drew in a lot of customers.

"Jaz mentioned you saw the killer." Gemma whispered as they entered the coffee house.

Gemma knew Jael's secret, and in time she'd have to tell Jaz too. Gemma wasn't thrilled on keeping it from Jaz to begin with, and now that Jaz and Cleg were working together on cases it would eventually come out. Better now than later when it could cause hard feelings.

Jael waited until they ordered their coffee and made their way to a quiet corner before saying anything. "The victims' spirits came to me, it's how I was able to describe the killer. Cleg told Henningsen so he'd agree for me to sit with the artist, but Jaz doesn't know yet. I guess he's been told the same story the artist got."

Gemma sat there sipping her coffee. "Are you going to tell Jaz the truth?"

She ignored her coffee, suddenly uninterested. The thought of telling Jaz made her ill. Jaz was too logical to just accept it, she'd have to prove it to him before he'd believe it, and even then he might still have doubts. "I'll have to but right now there's more important things for them to deal with. Once this is over I'll have you both over for dinner and tell him. Okay?"

"Good. I hated keeping it from Jaz. Married couples shouldn't keep secrets."

"Shall I point out that you're not married *yet.*" Gemma and Jaz had been engaged for almost a year, but no wedding date had been set. Right after he proposed she had been promoted to ADA, and it hadn't been a good time for a wedding and honeymoon. "When are you two going to start thinking about a date again?"

"Soon." Gemma took another sip of her coffee and looked around the café. "You said before spirits are all around us. Are there any here?"

"Two."

"There are?" Gemma nearly dropped her coffee as she looked around again as if she could see them.

"That young man." Jael nodded to the man working on his laptop by the window, the coffee long forgotten. "His father is sitting across from him, telling him he needs to enjoy life more, not work it away like he did. To take a long weekend and enjoy his wife and son, that kids grow up too quickly. He doesn't understand why his son can't hear him."

"Will you help him?"

Jael nodded. "When he's ready he'll see my light and come to me." Jael looked at Joy, standing behind the counter with the usual friendly smile. Looking at her, no one would know there was a deep hidden pain she carried. "Joy's twin, Grace, is standing beside her. The coffee shop was their dream, but Grace passed away from cancer before the place opened. Her sister was the one who came up with the name, but for Joy the place is truly her sister's. Have you read building's dedication outside?"

"No. What does it say?"

"May Grace always reside here and in my heart." Jael looked at Joy again with the knowledge that Grace would never leave her sister. She'd remain an earthbound spirit until Joy drew her last breath. "No one even knew because Joy is a transplant to Crystal Falls. She moved here seeking peace after Grace's death."

Gemma's gaze was now on Joy, her lips curved into a frown. "Is there something you can do for her?"

"No, Grace refuses to leave Joy." Silence settled over them while Gemma finished her coffee. Jael was too tired to make small talk. She wanted to crawl into bed, preferably with Death, to cuddle and sleep before the shit hit the fan again.

Gemma finished her coffee and sat it on the table before them. "I should get back to the office. You promise to tell Jaz when this is all over?"

"You have my word, though I don't know if he'll believe me." Jael made a mental list of things she didn't want to do but would eventually have to, and nodded.

"Great." That cheered Gemma up considerably. "Stay safe, leave the criminal chasing to the police."

"I have no plans to go after him myself." Even as the words came out of her mouth she knew they weren't completely true. If she had an idea where the Pishacha was, she'd go if it meant saving another woman. What was one little Pishacha? According to Cleg and Death, he was nothing compared to what Lucifer would send next.

After Gemma left, Jael sat there for a moment mustering the energy to get up. Death stood watching her as if he'd like to lift her into his arms and carry her away. "You're exhausted. Let's get you away from people and I'll teleport you home."

She pulled her cell phone from her pocket and held it to her ear so that if anyone saw her talking they wouldn't think she was talking to herself. "These spirits I see wherever I go…what am I supposed to do about them? I can't just pretend I don't notice, and I feel awful they're stuck here. Can I help them?"

"As you told Gemma, when they are ready they will come to you. Until then there is nothing you can do. You can't force them to cross over if they don't want to."

"So I'm to do nothing about him." She nodded to the man with the laptop and the spirit of his father. "Does he even know he's…"

"Deceased?" He shook his head. "No. He had a heart attack five weeks ago."

"Five weeks?" So much time had passed, and the spirit didn't know he was dead.

"Time travels differently for spirits. They don't realize how much time has passed."

A young girl entered the café with her mother, waving happily to the woman behind the counter. At first Jael thought the girl was waving at Joy. It wasn't until she looked and found Joy had her back to the door, preparing a coffee, that Jael realized she was watching someone else.

"Does she see Grace?"

"Yes. Most children can see spirits. Where do you think imaginary friends come from?" Death raised an eyebrow at her.

Chapter Eleven

Jael sat on the rooftop deck in the cold air. It had been a long and tiresome day, but now she sat waiting for something to happen. The killer could be out there stalking his next victim and there was nothing she could do. For once she had a moment alone. Death had gone to scan Johnsonville Road in search of the Pishacha. As morbid as it sounded, she was eager for the next attack. It would be their best chance to trap the demon.

"Lucifer's spawn all alone. Where's your guard dog, little girl?" A scratchy voice called out from behind her, reminding her of nails on a chalkboard.

Every muscle in her body tightened, her brain screaming for her to run. If it wasn't the Pishacha, it was another demon after her. The sulfur smell wafting toward her left little doubt in her mind. Turning to face him, she found the man from the women's visions.

His black hair was shoulder length, coming to just above the collar of his flannel shirt. Opening her senses, she became aware that the man was human. All along they had suspected the demon had just taken the shape of a human, not actually possessed one. Death told her that once a person was possessed, even if the demon was removed they would never be completely functional again. The Pishacha had stolen this man's life as he had ended the lives of the women. Anger replaced her fear.

No more lives lost, this ends here and now. She called the ball of electricity to her hand.

"Oh, no you don't." He cast an invisible net over her, and she could feel the weight of it as her ball of electricity fizzled out. "I won't let you have the upper hand on me, Lucifer's spawn."

"What have you done to me?" She tried to bring the fire forward, but even that seemed dampened by the net.

"A magical confinement net, that is all. While you're in it you will not be able to use any of your abilities." He spoke with a lot more excitement than seemed natural.

"Looks like it's a stalemate then, since you won't be able to hurt me either."

"That's where you are wrong. You'll feel everything I dish at you and you'll be powerless to stop me. Killing the Mistress of Hell won't go over well with Lucifer, so I'll make it worth it." He stepped closer to her, waving his arms until he was able to gather the net into his hand. "Hold on." He snatched it like it was under her feet, and she fell. Before she could hit the ground everything around her disappeared in the sickly scent of sulfur and fire.

Mentally she screamed for Death, willing him to be able to hear her, to come for her before it was too late. If only she hadn't gone to the rooftop deck alone. While she thought he was out searching for the next woman, he was actually waiting until she was alone. She was his next victim.

She wouldn't go down without a fight. If her abilities were down, maybe she could use the physical skills Cleg forced her to learn when she became a paramedic.

Seconds later she was flat on her back with only trees surrounding here everywhere she looked. Alone, unarmed, and in the middle of the woods with a demon didn't bode well for her. She tried to push the fear away, to focus on how to get out of the situation, but it seemed almost hopeless.

"Here we are." He let out an evil laugh, his eye glowing red, the true demon peeking through.

"What do you want?"

"Want?" He laughed again, this time louder and longer. "I want what every demon wants, to kill. Lucifer has kept a short leash on most of the demons under his control but I will no longer be kept in hell, denied the delicious taste of human flesh. A fillet of fresh human, just slightly cooked until the outside has a tan and the inside is still red and bloody. There's nothing better."

Her stomach turned at the very thought. It was revolting to consider someone eating human flesh. The demon stood before her basically comparing her to caviar.

He closed the distance between them in two quick steps. "Unlike the others I won't drug you, I want you to fight back while I torture you. Once you're dead I'll cut away the finest pieces from your body for a dinner fit for a king."

Death!

A silvery string shot through the net, wrapping around her hands and tying them together before the web locked and dragged them above her head. He did the same to her feet.

"Must keep those out of the way, I know demons that would pay good money for your digits."

Her stomach heaved as she fought against the restraints.

I won't die like this.

She took a deep breath. Her fingers caught a string at the edge of the net and she began to pull. She tugged as quickly as she could, pulling and pulling, but it wasn't coming apart quick enough. The Pishacha snatched a knife that was strapped to his leg and dove at her. The web simply slid around his hand, allowing him through without creating an opening. He stabbed her in the stomach, just above her bellybutton, twisting the knife again before pulling it out. A searing pain coursed through her, bringing tears to her eyes.

As if by a saving grace, help appeared. Death popped out of thin air, his hand wrapped around Cleg's who looked a little pale. She forced her gaze away from them and drew the demon's attention back onto herself, giving Cleg a moment to adjust. The demon hadn't seen the new arrivals yet.

"That's not very creative of you," she snapped, forcing herself to sound harsh and accusatory. "People get stabbed in the stomach all the time and survive. You're going to have to do better than that if you really want to torture me. Make it worth it because you're going to bring Hell down upon yourself."

"I'm not scared of Lucifer."

Enough of the web fell away giving her room to move. She squirmed up just as he plunged the knife at her again, missing where he was aiming and catching her leg instead. Stars exploded in her vision, but as he pulled it out she was thankful the blood didn't begin squirting. He had missed the femoral artery.

"I meant Cleg. You don't seriously think that killing his twin would go unpunished?"

As she drew the demon's attention, Cleg had adjusted to traveling Death's way instead of through his normal means of fire and sulfur. Now that Cleg had gathered his wits, he threw a ball of fire directly at the back of the demon. The Pishacha screamed and rolled to the ground to put the flames out. It was just the diversion she needed to pull herself out of the web.

Death rushed to her, the spirit box in hand, as Cleg continued to throw fire ball after fire ball at the demon.

"He's asked us to wait," Death said. "He believes as heir he can kill the Pishacha. If not, we're to use the spirit box. Attacking you was a deadly insult, Cleg's within his right to kill him if he can."

"Cleg could be killed."

"He won't be. I told you before to open your senses and you'll see what happens, or just wait. Cleg is a natural born warrior." He wrapped his arm around her waist and drew her close. "I should have never left you." He kissed the top of her head.

"It's not your fault." She pressed her hand to her stomach, the blood trickling around her fingers.

"I'm glad you're going to be okay." He adjusted her so she was protected behind his body, so she could rest, leaning against him, exhausted from her fight and the wounds.

The Pishacha jumped off the ground, flames still covering his skin. "I'll kill both of Lucifer's spawns this night!"

Cleg said something Jael couldn't make out before throwing two more fireballs at the demon. Screeching echoed through the woods, flames growing brighter and higher.

"You are a demon of Hell. You will obey the commands of the heir forever. Coming after the Mistress of Hell will be the end of you." With those words Cleg tugged a string, tearing the demon from the man's body. In the shadows of the woods, Jael got a good look at the demon, but could only see a large black mass, glowing red eyes, and heavy silver chains covering his body.

"Now, Jael!" Cleg kept his attention on the demon.

"Hold the box with the lid open." Death thrust it toward her.

"We're going to bind him in this?" The wood was smooth under her fingers. For such a light box, the lid took more effort to lift than she expected.

He nodded. "Just hold it, I'll say the words." He moved behind her, tight against her back. "Brace yourself, he'll be pulled into the box with force. Are you ready?"

She was as ready as she was going to get.

"Demon of Hell, you will be an image of what you once were, a lesson to other demons. When they go astray there are punishments for their actions. For going after the Heir to Hell's throne and the

Mistress of Hell, the sentence is a condemnation to the spirit box to eternally suffer the tortures you inflicted on others. You're forever condemned to the spirit box, never to leave until your last remaining bit of your life is pulled from you, scattering your remains through Hell never to live again." Death's arm wrapped around her waist. "Demon Pishacha, into the spirit box to begin your sentence."

With those words the wind around them picked up, sending dead leaves flying through the air, and the Pishacha became a misty form, the chains still binding him. An ungodly scream echoed through the woods, shaking the ground under her feet. Then Jael could feel the box sucking the air in around them, like a vacuum cleaner over carpet, pulling the demon in with such force she stumbled backward. Death's embrace around her waist was the only thing that kept her standing.

As suddenly as it all started the lid slammed shut and the wind died. There was a lightness to the air that had been missing. An owl hooted in the distance, creatures returned to their normal nightly activates. Everything was peaceful. Until she looked at the man's body lying on the ground. After the Pishacha exited the body, it just collapsed. She wasn't sure he was still alive.

"He's fine." Walking to them Cleg answered her unasked questioned. "Sit the box on the ground." When she did what he asked, the same heavy silver chains that had covered the demon appeared around the box. "No one will be able to open this box besides the three of us. He'll suffer as his victims did, never able to fight back."

"You were winning, why didn't you kill him?" A few days ago she would have been insulted by the thought of killing a man, even a demon, but now she wanted the Pishacha dead. To bring a true justice for the victims.

"Since I couldn't get the demon to leave the body I had no choice. It would have killed the host, giving the Pishacha a chance to escape and find a new body and begin to kill again." Cleg nodded to the man behind them. "In the spirit box he'll never be able to harm anyone. For eternity he'll suffer through what he did to those women, and anything he did in his past to others. It's a more suitable punishment than death."

"What will happen to the host?" Now that the fight for their lives were over, the pain she had been pushing away came back with such force that even Death's touch only dimmed it. She adjusted, putting most of her weight on her uninjured leg.

"I have to take him in. His sanity is gone, he'll be in a mental hospital until the end of his days. There will never be a trial, but hopefully Maddie and the others can move on."

"We can." Maddie and the other women stood by the tree line. "You brought us the justice we needed, it's time for us to go."

"Let me heal you so they can cross through you." When she turned to look at him, Death explained without having to be asked. "You're the light, when the spirits are ready they cross through you. There's no pain or discomfort for you, but you will have to stand on your own. With me touching you they cannot cross through you. I'm only Death, nothing more or less. You, *kochanie*, are so much more."

"I won't make them wait any longer." She pushed away from him, determined to do this now. Leaving Death's touch, unbelievable pain tore through her, forcing her to stagger for a moment before finally gathering the strength to stand on her own. "Ladies, you were unbelievable. Sharing your memories, and not getting upset when I didn't know what I was doing. I'm sorry I couldn't save you. As you're ready, please go find the peace you deserve."

Shelly was first, she stepped forward and crossed through Jael without another look back at the women. Shelly's life passed before Jael, beautiful memories of being surrounded by a family and love, along with the crippling grief of losing her fiancé. Eagerness to see the man she loved was overpowering, bringing a smile to Jael's face.

The others passed through with much of the same effect, each of them having their own life and story told in a matter of seconds. Amber was the youngest, just beginning to live her life when it was snatched from her, but even she left with no regrets. It reminded Jael she needed to live each day to the fullest. Life was there to be valued not wasted away.

Maddie was the last to go, a touch of hesitation clear in her stance. "I just wanted to apologize. I was a little hard on you at the beginning. Actually, I was a bitch."

"Maddie, there's nothing you should apologize for. Dying as you did gave you every right to be upset. I'm just happy I could help you find the peace you needed."

Maddie stepped closer but stopped again a few inches from Jael. "You might have been green when I found you, but you're one rocking Grim Reaper. You should show off your rocking style with pink highlights like mine." Without further delay Maddie crossed through.

Jael couldn't help but smile at Maddie's life, it was just as she had expected. Living life on the edge, different colored highlights, but more pink than any other color. She let her unusual personality shine through.

After Maddie crossed over, Death wrapped his arm around her waist, his head resting against the top of hers. "Let me heal you and get you home." She turned into his body, cuddling against him. "You're an amazing woman, *kochanie.*"

She leaned against him, relieved it was over. This was the final nail in the coffin that was now her life. Her first assignment and she rocked it.

Chapter Twelve

Another day, another sun on the horizon, but this time Jael had finally made it home. Jeffery Black was in a cage, waiting for arraignment, and Cleg was in Hell taking the spirit box with the Pishacha in it.

With the Pishacha contained, life should return to normal, or at least as normal at her life could ever be now that she was the gateway for the spirit world. As far as she was aware Lucifer didn't know she had chosen Death, but it wouldn't be long before the next demon showed up trying to kill her. For now she was going to take advantage of every moment.

She stood watching the sun rise over the town, glistening off the river, and realized how much her life had changed. She could never go back to the woman she was before, she only hoped the woman she was becoming was better and that her mother would have been proud. Death came up behind her and wrapped her in his embrace. Her head rested against his chest, fingers intertwining with his.

"I think we should celebrate. After all, it's not every day we defeat a Pishacha and five women cross through me."

"What did you have in mind, *kochanie?*"

"You naked, in my bed." She spun around to face him. "Now."

He smirked, clearly amused. "We have all day."

"Then give it to me now, and we can have another round or two before the others get here this evening." There was a twinkle in her eye as she spoke those words. She refused to think about the impending doom of telling Jaz, but a promise was a promise, and at least Cleg was going to tell his side of things as well.

"I think that can be managed." He lifted her into his arms and dashed up the steps with her.

"We could have teleported." She teased as he placed her on her feet.

"Someone's getting used to her abilities rather quickly. Come on, let's shower. We're both have blood on us."

She watched him walk to the bathroom. Sex in the shower was a new thing for her, but knowing Death it would be memorable to say the least. She heard the water turn on as she stripped from her ruined clothes. Leaving them in a pile to be thrown away, she padded after him.

When she'd bought the building, the first thing she remodeled was her condo, especially the bathroom, and then worked through the rest of the place until it suited her needs and style. The bathroom was large, with a separate shower big enough for two. She slipped into the shower not waiting for an invitation.

Death stood with his back to the door, under the showerhead, soap running down his naked body. Her blood that had coated his skin was gone. Even though he didn't turn around, his back muscles tightened. For a moment, she stood there enjoying the way the soap bubbles slid over his body. Giving in to her temptation, she ran her hands up his slippery back.

"Took you long enough, *kochanie*. I almost gave up hope."

"I'd never leave you in here to scrub your own back, not with the implication of sex," she teased. She gently tugged his arm, pulling him closer. "When you came into my life I was ready to fight you with everything I had, but now I realize you were what I was looking for all along."

"I've searched centuries for you. It's truly amazing to have you in my arms, to know my search is over. I love you, *kochanie*."

"I love you too." She ran her hands over his wet chest.

Pushing her up against the shower wall, he crushed his mouth to hers, and slid his hand between her legs. Unerringly finding her core, he teased the bundle of nerves and dragged pleasure from her in hard, hot waves. She moaned around his unrelenting kiss. He held her captive against the wall, his fingers thrusting into her as his thumb continued to wring more pleasure from her core. Fierce desire rose within her like a tidal wave smashing through a dam.

"Death, I want you." She murmured against his mouth, holding onto him, wild delight ripping through her.

His teeth grazed her lower lip and he pulled his hand away. She cried out in frustration, but he ignored her demands. Gripping her hips, he lifted her and spread her thighs before he drove into her with one powerful thrust. He gave her no time to catch her breath before he began rocking in and out of her. She had no control as he left her mouth and kissed a path to her neck. Digging her nails into his shoulders she held on to him as every pump of his hips sent pulses of pleasure exploding through her. She came apart at the seams, her inner muscles clenching to him as he continued to drive into her.

He slammed home in a frenzy and his climax burst through as a second tsunami shattered her world. She shook with the force of it. If it wasn't for his support she would have collapsed into a heap on the shower floor.

When the water turned cold he shut it off, sliding free of her slowly and reluctantly. Her mind was almost numb, raw sensation skittering through her. Wrapping her in a towel, Death carried her out of her shower and dried her off. Her legs trembled, but she obediently followed him to the bed. For the first time since she was a child she felt completely content and safe.

Jael brought a pitcher of iced tea to the table where Gemma, Jaz, Nathan, and Cleg gathered. Death stood near the counter, but she didn't mention his presence. It would only excite and make Gemma nervous, and Jaz wouldn't understand, but that was about to change.

"Jaz, I know you and Cleg have had a rough week, with the murderer on the loose, so thank you for coming over tonight. I wanted to talk to you about something important." With a trembling hand she poured the iced tea. Would telling someone about her being the Grim Reaper ever get easier?

Gemma had taken the news reasonably well. At first, she'd thought it was stress from Jael's mother's death, but soon realized she wouldn't lie about something so serious. Nathan was much easier to tell since he had a hidden gift of his own and could see Death. Telling Jaz wasn't going to be as easy. As a police officer, he wouldn't believe her, and she didn't know how to convince him. *Here goes nothing.*

Lowering onto the chair between Cleg and Nathan, across from Gemma and Jaz, she glanced at Death, who gave her a subtle nod.

"Jaz, there is something you need to know about me. You've been told that I saw one of the murders."

He leaned forward, setting his tea aside. "Something about that never sat right with me. It was hours after the murder when she was found, but who am I to question Captain Henningsen. But we caught the man responsible, and he was just as you said he would be, so why does it matter now?"

"It matters because things like this might happen in the future and you deserve to know."

Cleg cut her off. "You deserve to know what Jael and I are."

"Whatever your secret is I don't care as long as at the end of the day the perp is behind bars." There was the Jaz that Gemma fell in love with, the one willing to help anyone in need. It's why he became a police officer. He had a heart of gold.

"You might not say that when we've finished." Her lips curled to a frown, and her stomach twisted into a knot. It was possible she was about to push one of her closest friends away. Jaz was like a brother to her and Cleg. Cleg met Jaz in the police academy and introduced her and Gemma. Their easy friendship and closeness might be a thing of the past after today.

"Well, out with it, don't keep me in suspense."

Gemma placed her hand over Jaz's. "Jaz, what Jael is about to say is going to sound bizarre, but just hear her out."

"She's right, and you probably won't believe me." Jael took a deep breath and spit it out. "I knew about the women's murder because their spirits came to me."

Jaz's eyebrows knitted in confusion. "What the hell are you talking about? What do you mean they came to you? How is that even possible?"

She didn't want to say those two little words, the ones that first sparked fear in Gemma's eyes. "It's hard to explain. I can tell you everything that happened to each of the women, describe every detail of them to you. I saw them."

"Cleg told you, or he showed you the reports and then you dreamt it. Maybe you're working too many hours. Maybe you should take a few days off." There wasn't much anger in Jaz's voice, just confusion.

"I told you it was ridiculous, but she's telling you the truth," Gemma said. "Jael is the Grim Reaper."

Jaz pushed from the table, nearly knocking over his iced tea. Cleg's quick reflexes saved them from having a mess to clean up.

"Damn it, Gemma, I was trying not to mention that." Jael shook her head. "I remember the fear that flickered in your eyes when I told you."

"I'm sorry. I was just trying to help." Gemma turned her attention back to Jaz. "Babe, please hear us out." She reached for him, but he pushed away.

"You knew?" Disbelief was clear in his voice.

"He told Maddie's parents, tell him about her mother clutching a pink and silver keychain and the engraving," Death advised Jael.

She rolled her eyes, thinking it wouldn't help, but tried anyway. "When you told Maddie's parents, her mother held a pink and silver keychain like it was the lifeline to her daughter. There was an engraving in the center. *You've always been and always will be my mother. I love you. Forever, your Maddie.*" When Jaz stared at her, she added, "Maddie was adopted. That wasn't in the case file, was it?"

"What?" Cleg asked.

"Maddie's biological mother and adopted mother were twin sisters, and she died in childbirth. Rose took the kid and raised her as her own." Jaz sank back into his chair as if the air had leaked out of him. "I didn't know when I went, it wasn't in the file. No one knew and since it didn't pertain to the case I promised I'd keep it close to the vest unless it was needed. How did you know, Jael?"

"Maddie was there as a spirit. When she crossed through me to the light, I saw everything." Jael gained more confidence now that Jaz seemed more willing to listen. "Maddie was the first one that came to me. Once I spoke with her and the others, I went to Cleg."

"What do these…spirits expect you to do?"

"I help…" She searched for the right words. "I help people move on once they've died. I assist them in finishing whatever business that's keeping them here."

"But this power only exists in the movies." Jaz clutched the table.

"She gave you proof that she's spoken to Maddie. What more do you need?" Nathan spoke for the first time since Jael began.

"You…you too? You know about Jael's power?"

"I can't see what Jael sees, but her ability has been proven to me in other ways." Nathan's smile was weak.

She was thankful he didn't say it was Death's presence that had given away her secret. Unlike Gemma, Nathan could see Death, but that wasn't always comforting.

"This is all so unbelievable." Jaz dragged his hand through his hair.

"While we're on the unbelievable…" Cleg paused, shooting a quick glance at Jael.

"You're part of all this as well? Do you see the dead?" Jaz looked at Cleg as if waiting for the other shoe to drop.

"No. Actually, I'm the heir to Hell." Cleg stated it as if he was telling someone there was milk in the refrigerator.

"The what?" A touch of alarm was in Jaz's voice, and even Gemma and Nathan stared at Cleg and Jael as their eyes widened with shock.

Cleg took a long drink of his iced tea before answering. "Our father is Lucifer. He has made me the heir and Jael is the Mistress of

Hell. I realize this is all hard to believe but you are our closest friends and we thought you should know. It's likely there will be some unusual things happening around us. If you want to distance yourself from us, now is the time, because before long our enemies are going to be lining up at the door for a piece of us."

Gemma reached across the table and wrapped her hand over Jael's. "We've been friends since grade school. I'm by your side through thick and thin."

"That means a lot. Thank you." Jael breathed a sigh of relief, the worry of losing her best friend slipping away.

"We're partners I'll cover your six anytime."

"Thanks, Jaz." Cleg nodded and rose. "How about Chinese? I'll order." Everyone seemed to agree with the food choice.

"Same with us, Jael. I'm not going anywhere." Nathan smiled at her.

Tension from the kiss still hung between them, and she had yet to tell him she was committed to Death. It was something she had to do in private, not with everyone gathered around. Until then she had to control herself, not send wanting glances at Death. The doorbell rang, pulling her from her thoughts.

"I'll get it. Captain Henningsen was stopping by on his way home to pick up the reports since I won't be going in tomorrow. I have business to attend to with Lucifer," Cleg explained before going answer the door.

"I still can't believe your father is Lucifer." Gemma shook her head. They both had gone through a wild stage in their early teens when it was all black clothes, and they even dabbled a little in witchcraft. Most of it harmless stuff, but they had read their fair share of literature on Lucifer and demons. Maybe that phase of her life would help to prepare her for the battle ahead. Somehow she doubted she'd ever be ready for what her future held.

Chapter Thirteen

Jael stood from the table, slightly lightheaded, and went upstairs to her loft. It was the only place she could go for a little privacy. Was there no place sacred from the ghosts? Could she not spend a night with her friends without a ghost barging in?

"You okay?" Nathan asked. He must have followed her without her realizing it.

"Yeah. I just needed a minute." She plopped down on her large king-size bed, grabbing one of the throw pillows and holding it. Death's scent drifted to her from the pillow, reminding her that this life was worth it to be with him.

"You saw something, didn't you?" When she just looked at him, he continued. "I know you did, so why even lie to me?"

She nodded. He was right; there was no reason to lie to him about it. She was tired and wanted to get rid of everyone, but Cleg and Henningsen were discussing business. Lou, another officer that had accompanied Henningsen, hovered nearby waiting for the Captain.

"Talk to me." He joined her on the bed. "What did you just see?"

"Lou's sister."

"His sister?"

She let out a deep breath. "Yeah. She had cancer and passed a few months ago. She's clinging to him, not ready to let him go."

"Maybe you can help her pass on?"

"I don't think so. She wants to be with him, to protect him. In his line of work, maybe he needs it."

"You can't help everyone. You know that, right?"

She nodded. "It's just so freaky."

"I bet. I couldn't imagine seeing people others don't. But it is a blessing, not a curse, and you have to realize that after today." Nathan ran his hand over her leg.

Death popped in and stood before her. "We could smudge the loft area with sage, which would prevent ghosts from entering."

"That would be nice. Then at least I won't have to worry about ghosts popping in while I shower." There seemed to be something extremely wrong with a ghost watching her bathe. "Later, though. Death, could you give us a moment?"

When he was gone, she turned back to Nathan. "Since you transferred from the fire department and took the place of my former partner, I wanted you to returned my affections. The easy flirting between us never seemed to go any further, until the other night."

"That kiss I hope will be the first of many more." His fingers teased up her thigh.

She wiggled out from under his touch and stood. "I'm sorry."

"You made your choice then?"

The disappointment was clear is his eyes. "It was somewhat pushed upon me, but it was the right one. Death and I belong together, we can do so much good."

Nathan rose off the bed and stalked to her. "With him, your life will be surrounded by death all the time. You'll be danger constantly."

"Nathan, I see spirits everywhere I look. I can't get away from that. There will always be danger, but either way I don't think Lucifer will give up without a fight. He needs to divide a wedge between Cleg and me." She refused to take a step back even when Nathan invaded her personal space. "I'm truly sorry, I believe we could have had something special between us if the timing had been different."

He just gave her a sad nod before stepping away and down the steps. She could hear his boots on the hardwood floors as he made his way to the front door and left. A piece of her wanted to cry as the last normal chance she had with Nathan left. Part of her wondered if in a few weeks' time she'd have to sit down with another partner and tell her story over again.

"You okay?" Death asked from behind her. She was so wrapped up in the loss of what could have been between her and Nathan that she didn't feel Death appear.

"I'll be fine. He was the last shred of normalcy in my life. Maybe it's for the best. Around me, no one is safe."

He came to her and placed his hands on her shoulder. "It won't always be like this. One day we'll have that peaceful life you always dreamed of."

"With spirits popping in and out? I don't consider it peaceful."

"Let's put it this way, without the danger that Lucifer holds."

She slipped her arms around his waist. "We just have to make it through living hell first."

"Yes, about that. Cleg is going to Hell for a few days. He's going to deceive the great deceiver and act the part."

She started to pull away but Death held her to him. "What do you mean?"

"Cleg is going to appear as if he wants to learn more about his duties if he accepts his destiny as heir. It will give us an insider to what Lucifer is planning."

"It will also put my brother in grave danger."

"*Kochanie*, you're both in grave danger as it is. Which is why Cleg and I have agreed on certain things. I swore I wouldn't tell you about his plans until after he left, and I promised I'd take you to Nightscape for a few days. We need time to work on your abilities, somewhere you'll be safe."

She strained to hear downstairs, but there was nothing. "Cleg!" She hollered, fear making the hairs on the back of her neck stand up.

"He's already gone. He's arranged for both of you to have a few days off, but he promises to be in touch. Either way, you can feel him, you know he's in no danger. I'll teach you how to communicate with him without relying on the phone or being together." He released her, but kept a hand on her hip. "Let's gather your things, and get you safely to Nightscape. We need you to be ready when the first demon attacks."

"Is Nightscape the safest option? After all, Abaddon is there."

"It will be fine. While we're gone I'll have Thunder smudge your loft. It will at the very least keep evil entities away from here. Most spirits will be deterred from it as well. There will be some who will ignore it, especially white spirits, the ones only seeking your help not revenge. The ritual will need to be repeated every six months."

If she wanted to survive, she needed to be ready, and that meant making sacrifices. First one was spending a few days in Nightscape working on her abilities. It would give Nathan time to adjust, and hopefully when she returned the tension would be gone.

Better yet, it meant alone time with the one man she wanted to be with the most—Death.

Marissa Dobson

Born and raised in the Pittsburgh, Pennsylvania area, Marissa Dobson now resides about an hour from Washington, D.C. She's a lady who likes to keep busy, and is always busy doing something. With two different college degrees, she believes you're never done learning.

Being the first daughter to an avid reader, this gave her the advantage of learning to read at a young age. Since learning to read she has always had her nose in a book. It wasn't until she was a teenager that she started writing down the stories she came up with.

Marissa is blessed with a wonderful supportive husband, Thomas. He's her other half and allows her to stay home and pursue her writing. He puts up with all her quirks and listens to her brainstorm in the middle of the night.

Her writing buddies Max (a cocker spaniel) and Dawne (a beagle mix) are always around to listen to her bounce ideas off them. They might not be able to answer, but they are helpful in their own ways.

She love to hear from readers so send her an email at marissa@marissadobson.com or visit her online at http://www.marissadobson.com.

Other Books
by Marissa Dobson

Clearwater Romance Volume One

As Fate Would Have It

Learning to Live

Learning What Love Is

Her Cowboy's Heart

Half Moon Harbor Resort Volume One

Restoring Love

Secret Valentine

The Twelve Seductive Days of Christmas

Praise:

And the plot thickens. I am really enjoying how the overall story arc of this series is going. There are so many players that it is fascinating to watch the plot unfold. Everyone's story is connected, but not in the ways that I had originally anticipated and that makes it all the more fun to read. ~ Delphina Reads too Much

Wow, Tigress for Two was everything I'd hoped it would be after reading some of Marissa Dobson's other books. She packed a whollop, enticing the reader with angst, suspense, romance and suspense...oh did I say that twice? Well good cause I meant to, because she did a great job of keeping the reader in suspense throughout the whole story. I never knew what was coming next but i was so intrigued I couldn't put the book down. I seriously never imagined mixing shifter species but it was done well. ~ A Passion for Romance

Stormkin Series

Storm Queen:

To use the word amazing is not too strong when describing this book. I've never read anything like it and I loved every minute of it. Do yourself a favor of buying this book, if you don't you'll be missing out. ~Rebecca Royce, bestselling author of the The Westervelt Wolves.

This was a great new addition to the paranormal romance world, it almost had a Urban Fantasy feel because the sex wasn't the main focus of the story and I LOVED that! I thought each scene was done

so well! I will be continuing this series! I can't wait for the next one!
~ Amazon Reader

Clearwater Series
Winterblom:

I found Winterbloom to be a sweet and delightful little romance. Ms. Dobson does a wonderful job of creating visual scenes that allow the reader to feel as though they are right there within the story. ~ Romancing the Book

Unexpected Forever:

Unexpected Forever made me cry. I'll admit it; I teared up quite a few times actually…Marissa has yet again written an amazing story full of emotions and detail. I totally recommend reading Unexpected Forever and other great works by Marissa. ~ Crystal Out There

Fate Series
As Fate Would Have It:

This book has all three of the Fate Stories in it! Each are about mountain lion shifters and finding their mates! All are sweet, Heartwarming, Romantic stories! I can't wait to read more by Marissa Dobson! ~Amazon Reader

Snowy Fate:

This was a very quick read, but with just a few pages, Marissa Dobson is able to get to the heart of this story. ~ Cocktails & Books

I really enjoyed Snowy Fate. I hope that you take the time to learn that no matter how hard you try you can't fight fate. ~ Books-n-Kisses

I thought this one was just perfect in length. There was enough background that I felt I knew the characters well and their attraction was believable. Fate has a way of making a HEA very real. I definitely recommend this one! ~ From the TBR Pile